Perfect Family

Perfect Family

Jerrie Oughton

Houghton Mifflin Company
Boston 2000

I gratefully acknowledge the guidance and suggestions and stories I received from the following friends: Marcia and Steve Jones, Paul Brett Johnson, Becky North, Janice Schweitzer, William and Jane Preston, Betsy Purcell, Jane McMillan and Ruth Paschal, Eddie Jones, Beth and Clay Vaughn and their mother. Dr. Martha Gurwitt often reads my work and offers suggestions and words of wisdom as she did with this story. As always our daughter, Cher, and my husband, Paul, enthusiastically read and encourage. Margaret Raymo, my editor, makes the difference between a story fragment and a complete novel.

When I began writing this book, I dug out all my high school yearbooks and read the comments my friends had written to me. You cannot see a group of people daily for a five-year period without learning from them. Though *every bit of this novel is fiction*, I drew on the many lessons and memories from the class of 1955 of Needham Broughton High School in Raleigh, North Carolina. Memories of those who, as of this writing, are alive and well, and of those who did not live to the year 2000 but are constant reminders of that last magic time:

Edwina C. Armstrong	William C. Hitchcock	Janet Lee Rice
Rita Jane Bennett	Frances Johnson	Eugene Rule
David A. (Bucky) Branham	Nancy Jones	Donald E. Small, Jr.
	Merton King	Enoch Lafayette (Nicki) Stamey III
William H. Brickhouse	Robert H. King	
Mary Frances Connell	Elinor D. Newberne	David Stephenson
Fred W. DeBerry	Frances Parrish	Robert W. Stewart
Paul V. Gainey, Jr.	Richard Ray	William E. Swain
Robert Hibbard	Shelby J. Raynor	

The text of this book is set in 11-point Palatino.

Library of Congress Cataloging-in-Publication Data

Oughton, Jerrie.
Perfect family / by Jerrie Oughton.
p. cm.
Summary: When Welcome, a fifteen-year-old living in a small town in North Carolina during the 1950s, finds out that she is pregnant, she faces some important decisions.
ISBN 0-395-98668-0
[1. Unmarried mothers — Fiction. 2. Pregnancy — Fiction. 3. Babies — Fiction.] I. Title.
PZ7.O897Pe 2000   [Fic] — dc21   99-054792

Manufactured in the United States of America
HAD 10 9 8 7 6 5 4 3 2 1

For Dale, who had nothing to do with this story and everything to do with family

There is only one history of any importance . . . the history of what you once believed and the history of what you came to believe.

—Kay Boyle

Part One

I

O VER NEAR THE EAST COAST, IN THE LOWLANDS OF North Carolina, is a small town named Lily. Small towns are notorious for counting on the sting of gossip to shape behavior. This was especially true in the 1950s and Lily was no exception. Gossip worked inside us teenagers, making us fear, according to the old adage, but for the grace of God, there we went.

"And that's why Lydia Meyers is leaving school. Leaving town," my best friend, Trudy Hampton, told me. "Said to somebody she only did it one time. One time!"

"Where's she going?" I asked.

"Nobody's saying, but you can bet she'll stay at least seven or eight months. When and if she comes back, it'll be with a little baby 'cousin.'" Trudy gave a knowing nod that put the finish on that conversation for the moment. Not for good, just for now. We'd get plenty of mileage out of Lydia Meyers's predicament. Although it only took her one time, if you could believe that.

We were "porch setting" on an April evening, Trudy and I. Not on my front porch but six blocks down on Main Street. On the front porch of Mrs. Canton, the new dressmaker in town. Porch setting, if you do it right, requires periods of quiet where you hear your own thoughts, building a head of steam for the next topic of conversation. We sat quiet, listening to a dog barking two blocks over. The sound was carried in a warm, softened way, not sharp like it is on November nights when the air's so cold that passage through it is clean and fast.

A car turned the corner onto Main and roared down the street toward the house where we sat. Screeched to a halt smack in front of us. The car door slammed and a shadow of a boy came our way.

He paused on the bottom step, taken aback by two strangers on what I guessed was his front porch. Raised his eyebrows, then grinned at the joke he was fixing to ask. "You professional porch setters?"

I didn't offer an answer. Didn't know what to say. We'd been sitting in rockers in the twilight waiting for Mrs. Canton to finish with my prom dress. She had to take it in some in the bodice. That was all. Fifteen minutes, she'd said.

"Why d'ya ask?" I said finally, looking the boy over. Trudy must have been struck dumb she was so quiet.

He sat down in another rocker. "Just wondered."

I kept looking. If he was Mrs. Canton's son, he surely wasn't one bit like her. Muscles pushed out his T-shirt and even by just the street and porch lights you could see enough to know he'd passed a few footballs in his time.

"Are you Mrs. Canton's son?" I thought I'd ask.

"Yep." He rocked slowly. "And you?"

I waited a minute to answer. Not sure if just my name would be enough. He hadn't given us his name. Or maybe I should state my business on his new front porch. New to him, at least. And to his family. Mama had heard a new dressmaker, real reasonable, had moved in not a mile from our house. Just six blocks down on East Main Street in the very opposite direction from us. Not being able to afford a fancy store-bought dress was no longer a problem. Making it was a lot cheaper. That was how I got a prom dress.

"My name's Welcome," I told him. And when he looked up to see if I was joshing him, I added, "Welcome Marie O'Neal. And this is Trudy Hampton."

He stopped rocking and looked me over. Just me.

Mom had let my sister, Evelyn Sue, pick my name. She'd been five at the time I was born. Said she wanted me to always know that, even though I was number three, I was certainly welcome. Never wanted me to forget it. Believe me, I've never once forgotten.

"Strange name." He started up rocking again but didn't take his eyes off of me.

And being as he'd not even given his name, I said, a mite ticked off, "What's yours?" Maybe to see if I could

3

gawk over his the way he was gawking over mine.

"Nicholas Canton."

He kept on rocking and looking. Mrs. Canton came to the front door, pushed the screen open, and said, "It's all done."

She had it hanging in a dry-cleaning paper as far down as it would go. The net skirt was too full, finally. Its whiteness picked up light like a corona around the moon. All flowing and misty. Even half in paper it was some kind of gown.

"You home?" Mrs. Canton said to Nicholas. "Eaten yet?"

He shook his head.

I thanked her and, as we headed down the porch steps, she called, "Honey, wait. Are you girls gonna walk all the way home in the dark toting that dress? Nicholas here'll give you a lift. You'll do that, won't you? And I'll heat up some supper while you do."

He said, "Where's she live?" like I wasn't even standing there myself. And I said I'd be just fine. Didn't really want to ride with him anyway. He wasn't the friendliest person I'd met that day. But his mama pushed it, so Trudy took off on foot for her house one block over and I laid the dress carefully across the back seat of his '51 Chevy and crawled up front with Mr. Muscle and off we shot.

And I do mean shot. He burned rubber in front of Mrs. Canton's front porch like hell was after him. My head whipped back, and I should have known right then and there this person was probably a bit strange, starting up conversations with questions about our being profession-al porch setters. Burning tires to the rim just driving up the street.

"Right up there on the right," I told him. "The white house with the wraparound porch."

"That one on the rise with the glass front door and the chandelier in the front hall?"

I nodded.

"Hardeeharhar," he said and drove right by it.

"But that was it." I had to tell him twice more before he'd believe me and turn around right in the middle of the street and deposit me and my twenty-dollar prom dress.

"Whew, Lordy!" he said, pulling his head back on his neck. "Didn't know I was bringing you home to a pure mansion."

Though we lived in one of the prettier, larger homes on the west end of Main Street, it surely didn't translate into wealth. It was a bargain when my folks bought it a quarter of a century ago and had allowed us to give the illusion of solidarity. Truth be known, we lived from paycheck to paycheck just like everybody else did. Daddy's real estate business had never actually boomed, just crept along keep-ing us afloat, but not a lot extra was ever forthcoming. It was the family name of O'Neal that set us up as pillars of the community. Been around for over a century.

Well, when Mr. Canton, Mr. Didn't-Want-to-Give-Me-a-Ride-in-the-First-Place, said that about our house being a mansion, I just ignored him. Hopped on out. Prayed he'd remember I had a dress in the back seat and hold still long enough for me to slide it out of there.

But, even after I'd slammed the back car door and was up on the sidewalk well away from his hot-rodding tires, he sat right there at the curb.

"Thank you," I said.

"You're welcome." Then he added, "Welcome." Like some kind of echo.

I stopped on the first step to the front walk. Looked back at him because he was still sitting there watching me. Maybe it was all those milk shakes I'd been forcing down twice a day that'd given me a little shape and form, finally made me have a figure. Maybe it was because I was wearing black. Always my best color. Or my hair with its henna rinse sort of caught night light.

But none of that. He asked, "What is that smell?"

That took me back.

"What smell?"

"Well if I knew," here he grinned, "I wouldn't be asking now, would I?"

I noticed his ears cupped out a little. Just enough so he wasn't drop-dead-in-your-tracks handsome. A girl wouldn't consider going out with a boy who didn't have a flaw or two.

I looked off to the side. *How'm I to tell him what he's smelling if I don't have a hint?* I saw our neighbor, Miss Wing, move a curtain at her living room window and knew it looked a bit funny to be stalled there in front of my house, shouting to each other about odors. And what was it he had gotten a whiff of anyway? I mean . . . was it food, or garbage? Was it the river across the street, with its close-to-the-sea smell?

"Oh. I'll bet it's the Cape jasmine bush," I finally said, glad I could help out. Glad to leave the very presence of this peculiar person. "Bye."

He watched me all the way up the front walk. Up the porch steps. To the door. There I turned around and waved him off. And he didn't leave any rubber on our street front either. Drove off right cautiously for a person who had torn up the street not five minutes before. Hot-rodding boy I'd probably never see again that spring of '55. The same spring when another boy, name of Elvis, was gearing up to snarl his way to everlasting fame, but most of us in Lily had barely heard about him yet. New name to us. So was Canton . . . Nicholas Canton. New name.

2

I FELT LUCKY TO BE GOING TO THE JUNIOR-SENIOR PROM. A lot of girls didn't have dates, Trudy for one. I thought a lot about Lydia Meyers and felt doubly lucky. There she was, somewhere far from Lily, plunked down in her shame, trying to wait out a baby. And here I was, going to dance the night away with a big, bad senior boy. Actually . . . a short, nice, regular guy.

Randy Newsome was president of the student body of Lily High School. He had been elected in the fall of my sophomore year, 1954, about a week before Hurricane Hazel had ripped through town. We'd all gathered for assembly, innocent as babes, not knowing a storm was brewing somewhere out there in the Atlantic off the coast of Cuba. There we'd sat in the auditorium to listen to the nominees make their speeches before we voted.

Big Man Jones got up. Harold was his given name. He

was our leading scorer on the basketball court and I felt sure he'd probably win the election. The speech he gave was passable. But, to tip the scales, his girlfriend had been giving out fudge in the halls of the school all that week. Wearing a sign that said, "Harold Jones won't fudge on you. VOTE JONES FOR STUDENT GOVERNMENT PRESIDENT." Front and back.

My daddy said he'd disown me if I ran around school with any signs pinned to my person, giving out free candy. "I'll be dadblasted if young people aren't going off the very deep end," he roared over the scrambled eggs Mama had whipped up for breakfast. Made me sorry I'd even shared that wee tidbit of my school life with him.

Grammie, who lived with us six months of the year, chimed in with her favorite phrase, "All going to hell and back in a handbasket." Every time she said that she ducked her head and looked down like mentioning hell was wicked and she was embarrassed at being so bold. But couldn't help it popping out of her.

My older sister, Evelyn Sue, was present at breakfast, but absent. Being twenty hadn't really made her an adult. She sat and stared into space an awful lot for somebody who was supposed to be a grown-up. And she had pictures of movie stars plastered all over the walls of her room. Hadn't settled on a favorite. But you could tell when she got all starry eyed, she was thinking of one of her movie stars. Daddy said she was *gaga*.

But Daddy's ranting that morning flew right over where

Evelyn Sue was resting, deep in thought I guessed, because she kept chewing and staring off out the window.

Daddy ate a few bites, then he flew back in with something about Frank Sinatra crooning out his songs like a hound dog with its tail caught in the truck tailgate. Personally, I thought he sang soft, like lullabies. Johnny Ray was the one who yowled. But, try to convince my daddy. Every chance Daddy got he tried to drag Frank Sinatra into it. Hated the very shoes that man wore. Would love to have blamed Sinatra, along with Eartha Kitt, for every ill the world was beset with.

And he always found some fault with me, too—the way I dressed or wore my hair. Seemed no matter how earnest my efforts, they were never enough. Not even close. My older brother, Julian, out on his own with two children and a wife, could do no wrong. Daddy would say, "Look at Julian now . . ." If I heard it once, I heard it a thousand times. I could never measure up.

Well, Daddy would have loved Randy Newsome's speech. In fact, did love it when I told him about it at supper that night.

"My kind of guy," Daddy had roared. "Uses everything God gave him and makes it work for him. He'll amount to somethin'."

Grammie and Mama both nodded, and I thought of a person in this tight family circle who maybe wasn't amounting to *something*. My daddy's version of *something*.

To be specific—Evelyn Sue. She was so starstruck with Hollywood, seemed she'd forgotten how to live right here in Lily. Vowed she wanted to take time off from her studies over at East Carolina College to decide on life. I guessed she wanted to find what to do with it. Life. I'm telling you, I might have been only fifteen, but I could tell something was in the wind with her. Ripe. That just named her state of mind perfectly. Ripe for trouble, as it turned out soon enough. I was surprised our parents didn't tune in on it. But then they were so busy criticizing her, they didn't actually take a moment to see her.

But Daddy did have a point. Randy Newsome had sure learned to use what he had to the best advantage. There old Harold Jones was, finishing up his five-minute speech. Smiling. Nodding at the applause.

Trudy nudged me when Randy walked to the lectern and we giggled because he was so short you could hardly see his head. Let's just make it easy here. Randy Newsome barely broke five foot three. He was the shortest boy in the senior class. Not bad looking but short.

Well, Randy got everybody's attention that morning when he suddenly turned around and walked back to where he'd been sitting. Now I was figuring he'd given up before he even got started, which, frankly, I would have done, being as speaking in front of five hundred people was not my favorite pastime.

But no. He stooped down and slid out from under his

empty chair a five-inch-thick volume of some kind, probably *Webster's Unabridged* he'd lifted from the library. Lugged it all the way back to the lectern and dropped it to the floor with a *thwack* that woke any sleepers up.

Then he climbed aboard and prepared to fly all over that auditorium. When he stood on top of the book and his head finally came into view over the top of the lectern, the whole place popped into sudden applause like he'd just launched for the moon or something. He wouldn't have had to say one word and still won the election hands down because his climb onto that tome said he didn't care whether he was short or not. That was the kind of thing that just didn't matter. Said Randy Newsome was worthy of being prez. He won it right there. You could just tell by the pained look on Harold Jones's face.

But, Lord, how the words rose from that dictionary, up, on through Randy's feet, up his legs, and right on into that boy's brain. He gave words a try in that speech that even teachers didn't know. He handed out words that inspired even the very dimmest person in that auditorium. And the next day? He won by a landslide.

Anyway, he was my ticket to the prom, though we'd never even kissed. I did tell Trudy the day he gave his on-top-of-a-book speech that I might think about kissing him soon, he'd made such a hit.

In my freshman year Randy and I had been in the fall play together, and I'd found out how funny he could be and he'd found somebody who would keel over laughing at his jokes and then turn around and top them. We had such a good time together that, on the spur of the moment, he'd asked me to the Christmas Dance and, though my parents didn't much like the idea of my dating a junior, since we were going with a whole group of people, they allowed it. And ever since, when we dated, it was always at least a double date if not three couples.

But the kiss finally happened that prom night in April. When I floated down our spiral staircase in that white net Mrs. Canton creation, with its red velvet cummerbund draping down onto one side like big drops of raspberries on a mound of vanilla ice cream, when I hove into view, Randy Newsome puckered up and—not yet, no kissing yet—whistled and won my daddy's undying support. Not to mention my grandmother's and my mama's and my older brother, Julian's, and his wife, Wysteria's, who had congregated to take pictures and see me off to my first junior-senior prom. They'd brought their two young-sters along to gawk, too. Took a picture of my corsage in its box. Of Randy pinning it on my dress. Of us standing side by side.

Evelyn Sue was absent and it hurt my heart. I wanted everybody there for my first really big dance. But she was off to the picture show. It was a movie called *East of Eden*, with this actor named James Dean in it. She'd only seen it four times already. Looked like she could have sacrificed this once. But no, she was as gaga over him as I'd ever seen her. Plastered his photographs and torn-out magazine pictures all over the walls of her room.

As it turned out, Julian and Wysteria didn't come just to take pictures. They came to our house to remember, and they never let a person get a word in edgewise, they were remembering so hard and fast.

"You remember that dance?" Wysteria said to Julian like the rest of us weren't standing around the room. "We weren't any more than on the dance floor good when the waistband elastic in my hoop popped. Slid right on down to the floor, too, I mean. I had to lean over and pluck it up off the floor and tote it over to the sidelines . . ."

I knew what came next. Had heard it so many times I could have thrown up, I was so sick of it. Wasn't about to let Randy hear that all the boys wore Wysteria's hoop like a lei around their necks, taking turns with it.

"We're off," I called, dragging Randy by the arm toward the front door. He'd sort of got caught up in Wysteria's story and would have stayed. I could tell. I thought I might have to say, "It's okay, Randy. I know how it ends and I'll tell you about it later."

"Why're you in such a rush, Welcome?" Randy stood on the top porch step and straightened his tie. "It isn't like a parade, over and done. They'll be dancing all night."

"Sorry." This was hard to explain. "Sometimes . . . families . . . get caught up telling stories, saying stuff."

My family was like that. So intent upon the past, they let the present slip silent for later use. Randy probably came from the perfect home, where people really listened to each other and built conversations from scratch. From the all-American family, with the mom sailing around directing traffic for her busy family full of successful people. "My son, the president of the student body, needs a dental appointment, please."

He turned to look at me and, in the moonlight, I could see his grin. Then he nodded at me.

"You're making fun of me, Randy Newsome..." I started, hotly.

But he held up his hand *no*. "No. I'm not. Believe me. Just this afternoon I had to take my eighty-seven-year-old grandmother to the grocery store and she told her life story to three people. Before we reached the check-out lane. Strangers, to boot."

I relaxed and grinned back. "Really? I thought my grandmother was the only one in town who did that."

"Not at all," he said and grabbed my hand to go down the front porch steps.

It helped. Made me think that Wysteria and her communal hoop might not be the hot topic at the next student council meeting. Behind my back.

"I'd like to meet your grandmother sometime," I said as he held my car door open and then stuffed my hoop and skirt in after me.

"Hold on," he shouted as I leaned far over behind the steering wheel and held myself tight together.

Randy slammed the car door and I sat back erect, knowing full well that if anybody were to open my door without warning, my dress would spring out at them like a wild animal, I was stuffed in so tight.

My hoop stayed in place, the Cape jasmine bloom I'd tucked in my hair trailed its sweet scent everywhere I turned, and I danced every dance. Maybe Randy Newsome wasn't a knockout like that boy Nicholas Canton, but he sure could crack jokes, and the evening flew by. After the band played newer songs like "Little Things Mean a Lot" and "Hey, There" and "Young at Heart," they finally played "Good Night, Sweetheart," which is the eternal signal that it's over. I'd learned that at earlier dances. Not big proms like this one, but the Harvest Dance and the Christmas Dance.

When Randy drove me home, we parked out front and talked about the music and the decorations, which I thought hid the fact we were in a gymnasium. He said it wasn't perfect though, because you could still see the basketball hoops sticking out above the palm trees, and every time he'd almost believe he'd escaped to the Isle of Capri, those confounded basketball hoops brought him right back to Lily High School and a gymnasium where he'd never been able to play basketball. Being prez of the student body was, admittedly, something, but all things considered, he'd just as soon have played basketball, thank you very much. And I said I'd rather he be prez and smart and that's when he looked at me like he was taking me in for the very first time. Then he leaned right over and kissed me on the mouth.

It wasn't a long one. But it was my very first kiss, and it was nice. Comfortable, like Randy. I was two inches taller than him, so it was good we were sitting down. Maybe he'd get a growth spurt or I'd quit one. Who knew?

3

THE FAMILY I GREW UP IN, WHILE NICE ENOUGH AND I'm sure down deep loved each other amazingly, on the surface set out a number of road signs to distract a person. I guess Mama and Daddy wanted the three of us, Julian, Evelyn Sue, and me, to be as near perfect as possible. They were always teaching. Giving examples from their pasts. "When I was young and the dinosaurs roamed the earth," Daddy would begin, and I felt like rolling my eyes back in my head to bear hearing whatever he'd say next.

And Grammie, she made a person want to hide from her. Telling how she taught piano for fifty-two years, arranged flowers for every funeral that the Centenary Presbyterian Church held between 1900 and 1945. What did that have to do with me?

Here I was, trapped in a body that was trying to survive my fifteenth year and Mama tried to soften it for me with stories about *her* fifteenth year. The only good thing I could think of was I'd survived being fourteen. Last year I had grown too fast, so I had hit ninth grade with legs as big around as pencils and was taller than most of the boys. My hair had a will of its own, and I hadn't discovered make-up yet, so my eyes were two brown seeds that got lost in a very plain face. Even my smile was crooked and too wide. I know they say the inner person is what counts, but the people who are saying that are all adults who live in less awkward shells. When the casing is so imperfect, it's really hard to even find that inner person.

Now that I was almost sixteen and my shell had suddenly smoothed and was gleaming, so to speak, you'd think the inner being would unfold and spread to fill its exterior. Not so. Inside I was still fourteen and awkward as a goose. Maybe that would never change. Maybe all my life I'd always be a crimped fourteen in my heart.

I did feel a little older two weeks before Randy graduated that June of '55, when Evelyn Sue and I had our talk. Older maybe, but not much wiser. Maybe just more open to hurt. Perhaps that's what happens as you get older. There's just more and more of you open to hurt.

I found out where Evelyn Sue was coming from and where she was going about a week before Mama and Daddy did. No wonder. They probably wouldn't have listened to her if she had opened up and tried to tell it. Would have cut her off at the pass with their own stories.

Evelyn Sue was packing a suitcase she always kept out

of sight under her bed, her large suitcase, when I strolled upstairs.

"Going somewhere?" I asked as I stood at the bathroom door that separated our two rooms.

"You might say that."

I watched. Didn't go in. Just watched and noticed right away not a picture of James Dean was left on the walls. Even the one on the ceiling right over her bed was gone.

"You've always liked this sweater, Welcome. It's yours." She held out a blue cashmere sweater she had gotten last Christmas. I didn't hesitate. I had to go into her room, though, to get it.

"Thanks," I said, surprised. Evelyn Sue never gave much of her stuff away. Held on to things she never even used, just in case, I guessed. "Where you goin'?"

"Far away."

I leaned against one wall and watched. "Does Mama know?"

She was folding a pair of jeans and she stopped and looked at me. "Not yet."

"Hadn't you better tell her?"

"I will. Pickin' my time. That's all." She knew I'd never tell. Never was much of a tattletale.

She packed awhile before she said, "It's really hard. What I have to tell. Hard." She hit the *d* with her tongue on the back of her teeth and I felt the hardness.

"I'm going . . ." Then she stopped like I'd know where.

Waited. Corrected herself. *"We're* going to California to find James."

I watched to see if clues would materialize. Didn't.

"Who's we?" I began.

"Sandy, Glover Williams, and me."

"Who's James?"

"Dumb!" She spat the syllable at me like I had sponge for brain matter. Then looked at me with the slightest nod of her head to force the brain waves she was sending in my direction. When that didn't work, she said again, "James." Then, "James Dean."

As her words found home, my knees sort of gave way, and I slid down the wall and squatted on the floor. I might be thick as a plank and need remedial conversation to keep me abreast of what she was saying, but I did know she had finally left her sanity somewhere behind. Going to California to find James Dean? Shoot! She was suddenly way off the beaten path here. Yes. She really was. Heading for whatever roads took a person west from Lily, on across the continent of North America until they hit the Pacific Ocean.

"Why?" I whispered it because I had never actually been in the presence of an insane person before and didn't want to throw her totally out of kilter with too many questions. I'd start small and build.

Evelyn Sue stopped packing. "Because . . . I am in love with that boy."

I remembered the pictures that no longer filled her walls. Tried to remember him. *Let's see*, I told myself, *he squints, rides a motorcycle, wears a leather jacket, has blond hair . . .*

"If you find Marlon Brando instead, will you call me?" my voice asked in a halfhearted attempt at humor.

"Sure," she said, serious as death, and turned and sat beside the suitcase. The sudden movement of the mattress flung the lid down on her half-packed life.

"What're you gonna do if you find him?" I asked, sinking lower to the floor for comfort.

She shrugged. "You've never been in love, Welcome, so you can't understand."

She was right about one thing. Actually, two: Hadn't been in love. Didn't understand. Nope.

I held the secret almost a week before Mama knew. The day Evelyn Sue took off and left a note, Mama held it all of three minutes until she could reach Daddy on the hall phone and they went crazy together. Mama took to her bed and Daddy threw things, like shoes and curse words. I stayed well away because their anger ate up air.

And, as much as anything, it was because of what people would say. That was Mama's one-liner. Over and over. *Forget what people will say*, I thought. *Worry about Evelyn Sue. What's going to happen to her? Way out there in California!*

I didn't start missing her until about two weeks after she'd gone. And by then my question was this: was it bad she made the choice to go in search of Eden, of a dream?

Or did it seem so bad because she'd be the subject of half the conversations I'd hear at school in the girls' bathroom? A lot of Evelyn Sue's friends had younger sisters in high school. Here she'd gone traipsing off after a movie star. In the company of two friends, one of them a boy. People all over town would tell it and point at me and whisper. Point at me. Me! And I had absolutely nothing to do with this choice. Yet I'd be the one to catch the flak because I was still here in Lily and was the sister of somebody who'd suddenly gone loony. There it was! I was beginning to think like Mama, caring what people said. Not worrying about the real problem, Evelyn Sue.

In small towns all across the South that spring, there was probably a thin trickle of boys and girls who left home in search of far-fetched, impossible dreams. Evelyn Sue was the only one I knew, though. At night in my bed, I stared up at the paisley bed canopy moving gently with the suction of the ceiling fan. Prayed Mama's predictions wouldn't come true. Prayed she wouldn't turn wild as a hurricane and land back here pregnant with God knows whose baby taking hold inside her. Prayed she'd be safe and find Eden at least, if not James Dean.

4

For baccalaureate service, my entire family (except for Evelyn Sue, of course) trooped over to the First Baptist Church. Nobody we were kin to was graduating, walking in wearing a dark cap and gown. We did know Randy Newsome, and he was going to speak as president of the student body. That was something right there. But not enough to bring Daddy out on a Sunday afternoon. No, it was my singing a solo of sorts.

Our a cappella chorus was doing two numbers, "Swing Low Sweet Chariot" and another spiritual called "Righteous Is the River," which had a part for a girl to sing that reached higher than the stars and a solo for a bass. We'd all tried out, *auditioned*, Mr. Whitmore called it. When it came time for me to step up beside the piano and hang by my fingertips, I did so. Never faltered. Hit every one of those high notes Mr. Whitmore struck, square on, and Mr. Whitmore sort of smiled. Next day he said I had the solo.

So the O'Neal tribe trooped to church. I wore a sundress under my choir robe to beat the heat generated by forty-two bodies standing close together in the choir loft.

We sang "Sweet Chariot." Sat and waited through four speeches. Randy's was one. This time he didn't stand on a book, but the words still came. He told how he would always be remembering these past four years of high school. Said there were teachers who'd changed the course of his life. I'll have to admit, my mind wandered a little. Well, a lot. I suddenly started thinking of Nicholas Canton. Hadn't given much thought to him since the night he drove me up the street. But somehow he popped into my head. Danger was written all over the boy. So I pushed him on out of my mind.

Randy finished speaking, stepped back, and sat in his seat on the stage. Mr. Whitmore stood and turned to us. We rose up like we were all part of one body. Had even practiced that part a hundred times. Ward Johnson, the bass soloist, made his way down to a microphone. Then there was silence and stillness. With the signal we blasted out like thunder, "Righteous . . . Righteous is the river," basses carrying the load.

When my part came, the altos and sopranos were singing soft and I began my climb. On my last note, there wasn't a sound but my voice, hanging a note so pure and lofty I figured chandelier bulbs might be bound to explode. I did it twice and Ward Johnson hit his notes hard and rich in between. I took pride in not needing a microphone, though.

At Mr. Whitmore's signal, we ended those last words— *take me home*—with a fraction of silence.

The audience burst into applause and jumped up from the church pews. It went on for a long time. Long enough for me to find my family and see them beating their hands together, my daddy, my mama with her program nailed under her elbow. Grammie, the flowers on her hat springing along with the thunder of her hands. But my daddy most of all. A grin as wide as the state of Texas. It was a pure pleasure to watch.

I missed Evelyn Sue not being there, but Julian and Wysteria were. And their kids.

And I wouldn't mention any of this except that it marked, like a bookmark, the first time I thought I might fly after all. Not literally, but it seemed at that moment that something new might have entered me. A believing I might be able to do or be anything I wanted. It might be possible. And I hoped in years to come, I'd always be able to go back to this page and spread my dreams out around me and let them carry me.

5

THE LETTER CAME TO ME THE MORNING I WAS GOING with Mama to her DAR meeting. School was out, and I reckoned Mama thought I needed some social training so I'd grow up knowing how to act.

"Run get the mail," she'd said while she stabilized her hat at the hall mirror.

I saw it right away. Tucked it into my dress pocket for later because it was addressed to me and it was from California. It stayed hot next to my leg all through the luncheon meeting, burning a sweet hole in my pocket. It wasn't that I didn't want Mama to read it; I just didn't know yet. In the first place, it would hurt Mama's feelings that the letter was for me, not her. I would read it, and then see if I dared share it around. It was the first letter to arrive from Evelyn Sue.

The DAR meeting lasted until two in the afternoon . . .

well, two-thirty by the time we'd said our good-byes.

"Can I stop off at Tayloe's Drug Store?" I asked Mama when we turned down Market Street.

"Well, how'm I gonna do that?" she asked, looking over at me from under the brim of her white straw hat. "Main Street's one way down at that point. You know that good as I do."

"Yes," I said, "but you could let me off at the last corner as you turn onto Second Street. That way I'll only have a block to walk instead of four and a half from the house."

She drove on at a good clip, open window–wind taking what hair had escaped her hat and feathering it around good.

"What are you gonna do at the drugstore?" she wanted to know. "Can't be hungry after that big luncheon."

"No'm. Want to buy a *Modern Screen* . . ."

"You know how your daddy feels about that, Welcome Marie. He vows movie magazines are a waste of your time and money." She looked over at me with her dark, quick eyes. Mama never looked long at a person, like she knew the power of her eyes, that they might pierce clear through somebody. Just a glance was enough.

"That's the same thing he said about comic books," I said. "'It's *my* allowance."

She sighed a huge breath. The way I figured it, Mama was so shell-shocked over Evelyn Sue she'd pretty much give in over small stuff so she didn't lose me, too. Then all she'd have would be Julian and Wysteria and their two

28

kids, and God help her if that's all she'd have left from a family of three children.

Evidently she thought so, too, because just after we'd turned right at the First National Bank, she swung over to the curb and pulled to a stop.

"Don't you spend the whole afternoon there now, you heah?"

I nodded. Tried not to slam the heavy car door but still close it shut. Watched her drive on down the street before I crossed.

Main Street in Lily was one block removed from the river. So every store had to rebuild and start over about once every twenty years. Because when the Pamlico River rose, watch out. People paddled down Main Street in fishing boats and canoes. When the waters receded, some of the businesses threw in the towel. New ones sprang up: dress shops, a music store, cafés.

Tayloe's Drug Store always stayed. So did the theater and the two jewelry stores. Main Streets, the lifeblood of small towns, housed three-quarters of a town's businesses. And Tayloe's Drug Store, being the oldest besides the two banks, had people working there who'd been breathing air back before the turn of the century.

Tayloe's was a dark store despite a bank of fluorescent lights beaming all the way along the ceiling from the front to the rear, where you could enter from the back parking lot if you wanted to get in that way. The darkness was inevitable because the ceiling was at least thirty feet high. A stray bird or two flew around up there, it was so high. Mr. Gravely Tayloe, perched on a tall stool behind the counter, surveyed the comings and goings of his customers. Speaking and nodding to people. Spying. Too old to do much else but rest his gartered shirtsleeves in the hollow of his concave stomach and pass time. Probably gas, too, truth be known.

I purchased a milk shake and *Modern Screen* at the counter. Went over to a booth on the wall, beyond the four tables, and pulled out my letter from Evelyn Sue. I unfolded the envelope and tore the end off like I'd seen Mama do to every letter she ever opened. Then I slid the letter out and opened it up.

Dear Welcome, it began. I took a sip of milk shake through the paper straw and read on.

> *This is just to let you know a new mailing address in case of an emergency, in case Mama or Daddy were to die.*

I took another sip.

> *It's very different in California. Can't say that I like it yet. Sandy and I have met lots of people in the four weeks we've been here, but not many I would really want to be close friends with. I guess that'll come.*
>
> *Before I forget it, my new address is: 14 Oak*

Street, Apt. B, Los Angeles, California.

Seven of us live in this side of an old house that's about seen its last days. I hung my pictures of James Dean over the holes in the walls to fix it up a little. And you remember that flowered skirt of mine you always wanted to borrow and I wouldn't let you? Well guess what our bedroom curtains are?

"Got a letter from your sweetheart?" a voice over my head asked and, instinctively, I pulled the letter to me and looked up.

It was that hot-rodding Nicholas Canton looking down at me, grinning like we were best friends, when all we'd ever done together was tear up to my end of Main Street one evening in his '51 Chevy.

"Oh, hi." And the letter went right back in my pocket.

"It *was* from your sweetheart," he said and slid in the other side of the booth like I'd invited him. "Mind if I sit here?"

I shook my head, then took a sip of my milk shake.

"You're mighty dressed up for a Tuesday afternoon. You always wear Sunday dresses around town or . . . are you expecting somebody?"

"Nope." Nope to what? I'd already forgotten but it was what I'd found at the tip of my tongue, so out it came.

He just stared and grinned. Had dark hair that curled where it ended, curled right up against his neck. And his grin, though shy, still knew its strength. He wasn't about to waste it where it wouldn't count for something. "My mama said you sang like a bird at church Sunday afternoon."

"What was she doing there?"

He shifted in his seat. "Got a cousin graduated. You know Silas Canton?"

I shook my head.

"A real quiet boy."

I drank some more. The silence bothered me more than it must have bothered him. Finally, just to have words moving around, I said, "I'm wearing this dress because I went to a DAR meeting with my mama."

He frowned. Started to ask, "D . . . ," but had to clear his throat. " DAR. What's that?"

"Daughters of the American Revolution, I think," I said.

"One of those lah-de-dah society shindigs?"

"I reckon."

I sipped away and suddenly a laugh came upon me so strong I nearly choked.

"What?"

I smiled to hold in the gut laugh that wanted out. "It was definitely lah-de-dah. Left me right out in the cold. I know my mama'll probably never ask me to go again. They may even ask *her* not to come back after all that went on."

He sat, smiling just enough to encourage me to go on, to open up so we wouldn't be stuck in silence. So I did.

"When we first got there," I said, "and it was in one of

those *real* mansions down off River Road on the way to the country club, I needed to go to the bathroom, which I found easy enough. It was just getting out of that little closet of a guest bathroom that got to be a problem. The door jammed and wouldn't open back up."

He sucked in a breath that must have filled him with humor because he nodded and grinned big. "You spend the entire meeting in the privy?"

"No. At first I hopped up and down trying to shove the door where it was stuck. Nothing. I could hear the ladies, about twenty-two of 'em, all squawking and squealing like a yard full of ducks. Finally, I knocked on the door."

Nicholas threw his head back to look at Tayloe's high ceiling and laughed a hard, boy laugh.

"The hostess, Mrs. Smithwick, walked right by my jammed door, and must have looked on out her front door. I heard her say, 'Well, I declare I heard somebody knocking,' all wondering, like they'd disappeared into thin air.

"'It's me,' I called. 'Welcome.'

"'Welcome?' she echoed back. 'Where are you?'

"'I'm stuck in your bathroom,' I shouted.

"'You're where?'"

Well, at that Nicholas put his head down on his arms and howled like a hunting dog. It was pretty funny, now that I was away from it. Even when he quit howling he kept his head down, hidden in his arms.

"Well," I continued, "she finally figured out where my voice was coming from and, between the two of us, we uncorked the door and out I popped."

Nicholas said from where he still rested, down on his arms, "Please tell me that was all."

"Yep," I said, finishing off my milk shake with a loud, hollow suck. "If you don't count they nearly had to call an ambulance at the end."

He looked up. "What happened?"

"Mrs. Smithwick had all these little sandwiches and cheese and fruit laid out in crystal and China dishes on her cutwork tablecloth. And to drink, she had this frothy green punch in glass cups that matched the glass plates. We ate first; then they started the program. Well, I kept my second cup of punch with me where I sat with Mama, over by the baby grand piano."

"There's a dangerous situation right there," he said, stretching and shifting his legs.

"You're right. I should have let the maid take it on into the kitchen. Actually, I should have followed her into the kitchen and helped her wash up the cups and plates. But I didn't. The program was about sunken treasure."

Nicholas perked up, interested.

"A man who dives for treasure gave the whole thing. Lives right down in Beaufort . . ."

"Wouldn't be Othello Duckett, would it?"

My mouth flopped wide. "Well, how did you know?"

"I've read about him in the paper. Said he's been hunting Blackbeard's sunken ship for several years."

"That's the very person who it was," I said, "and what he

had to say and show was really interesting. He had real gold coins he's recovered, doubloons, he passed around . . ."

"Reckon your mama could wrangle *me* an invitation to the DAR next time?" he asked all wide-eyed and full of himself. We laughed. "So, when did the ambulance part come in?"

"Oh, well Mr. Duckett just got married about a month ago and, after the program, the ladies were asking questions. Informal like. 'Do you live on the boat?' 'Ever get seasick?' I was just getting set to take a long swallow of my green punch when a little lady, up front, with blue hair, said, 'Tell us about your new wife, Othello.'

"He didn't hesitate a lick. I had a mouthful of punch heading down when he popped back. 'Well,' he said, 'she's built like Marilyn Monroe and, for my money, she's a whole lot sexier.'"

Nicholas whooped. "You know he didn't say that to all those little old ladies!"

I nodded. "Said it right there in front of God and twenty-two DARers. And my drink of punch went down the wrong way. I didn't reckon I'd ever be privileged to fill my lungs with air again. Thought my last view of life would be the legs of that baby grand piano. It was like trying to breathe underwater.

"'Lift your arms up over your head,' Mama whispered, and I did, but help was slow in coming. A lady sitting in back of us warped me between the shoulder blades, which nearly knocked me out of my chair."

"Warped?" Nicholas asked.

"Yeah. Whacked me good across my back."

Nicholas shut his eyes and laughed all inside himself. Shook his head.

"It isn't that funny," I told him, but he said it was and kept right on laughing.

Finally, he wound down and said, "I swear, Welcome O'Neal, you're 'bout the funniest woman I have ever met."

And all I got from that? The one word, *woman*. *Funniest* spun right on by. It was Nicholas calling me a woman that punched a button deep inside of me and skidded me to a halt like bare feet on velvet.

I guess my watching him all solemn finally slowed him down. "You reckon you'd like to take in a movie one night this summer?" he asked me.

When he focused on my eyes, it was like we were locked together. Nobody, not old Mr. Tayloe spying on us, could have tapped in on that connection.

"I reckon," I said at last, and he walked me home from Tayloe's Drug Store and sat beside me in the swing at the corner where the porch wraps around, and Mama came out along about six o'clock to say dinner was set and I introduced her to Nicholas and later she said he didn't look to her like our kind of people and besides was much too old because he shaved, but it was too late by then. He was already in my head. And anyway, I told her, Randy shaved. You just couldn't tell it because of his red hair.

At eight I called Trudy and told her all about Nicholas Canton. We talked for forty-five minutes, until Daddy hollered for me to get off the phone so any other callers would stand a chance. It occurred to me, after I griped silently, that I might be the one getting a call, maybe from Nicholas Canton, so I hung up quick.

Along about nine I sat on the floor under my open bedroom window, smelling the Cape jasmine, and began to read Evelyn Sue's letter again, picking up where I left off.

> There's not any furniture, to speak of. I'm still sleeping on a sleeping bag. Sandy hauled in a mattress she found at the curb, said sunning it would be enough to kill any germs or bedbugs. No thanks! I'll stick with my sleeping bag.
>
> We haven't been able to catch up with James Dean yet. Word is he's down in Texas making a movie named Giant. But he can't stay there forever. I figure, eventually he's bound to come home. I've got to say this whole experience has taught me a thing or two. That old saying, "Look before you leap," has new meaning somehow. If I'd known he was in Texas, I'd have headed south instead of west.
>
> Well, take care of yourself and write me sometime.
>
> Evelyn Sue

She added a P.S. and gave an emergency number to call her at. I decided Mama didn't need to know about grimy mattresses and holes in walls, so I put the letter in my underwear drawer, back down behind my stockings and garter belt. Of course, its being there geographically didn't necessarily mean it was gone from my mind. I did wonder if Evelyn Sue meant she was regretting that she'd gone.

And now what? If she wanted to, could she come back home? I mean, as Robert Frost's poem says, family's where you turn when there's no place else to turn and they're bound to take you in. Mama and Daddy were still so mad, though, would they?

6

Mama's saying Nicholas Canton wasn't our kind of people sort of sent up a red flag. For me, the red flag only meant don't bring him home anymore. Should have meant kiss that boy good-bye and concentrate on something else. But I now thought he was the most compelling boy I'd ever known.

He called two nights later.

"Welcome," Mama crooned. "Phone's for you."

"Hello."

"Hey. This is Nicholas."

I swallowed hard and calmed my breathing. "What you doin'?" I asked.

"Not much of anything. Just sitting around."

I glanced at Mama, who was lingering, picking dead leaves off the fern by the front door. This was awkward enough without an audience. Randy Newsome had almost never called. We'd always set things up at school. And now he was gone for the summer to be a counselor at Camp Seagull. Some other boys called but not anybody I really wanted to date. A few I wouldn't date if my last day on Earth were set for tomorrow. Mainly girlfriends called. Mostly Trudy.

"I was wondering," Nicholas said, "if you'd be interested in going to a movie with me." Some people say *intristed*. And then there are some who say *inte-rested*. Nicholas said it like that, pressing on that next-to-last syllable. You could tell he'd moved here from somewhere else.

"What's on?" I asked, and Mama moved around to the other side of the fern, plucking some more and stuffing dead leaves into her apron pocket.

"Marlon Brando's in something. I don't remember what."

"When?" Nothing like getting to the point.

"How 'bout this evening?"

"Can't."

"Well . . . I work construction tomorrow. Going out River Road. We're bricking up a house. How about . . . tomorrow evening?"

I looked at Mama. A fern sure hung on to a lot of dead leaves. Shouldn't. She misted it three times a week. "I don't think so." I knew Mama would never agree to me going to a movie with the likes of Nicholas Canton. And I couldn't say much of anything with her hovering so close. But he took the bull by the horns.

"Tell you what. The first day it rains and I don't have to

work construction, I'll call and we'll make plans then. Maybe take in a matinee. Okay?"

"Sounds good to me. Bye."

After that, I jumped up quicker than a cricket every time the phone rang, rain or not. And wouldn't you know, it didn't rain for seven straight days. Finally came a day when it poured from early morning on, and along about ten in the morning the phone jangled. I'd been hanging close by. Mama was upstairs vacuuming, so I had the privacy I'd not had that first phone call. Two forty-five P.M. at Tayloe's Drug Store. The theater opened at three.

I struck out about two-thirty, toting an umbrella and wearing a raincoat over the top of my shorts. Told Mama I was heading over to Trudy's. Took me nine minutes to walk it and I bought a movie magazine. I didn't want to appear anxious, so I just perched in a booth and thumbed pages and waited. He was right on time.

To this day I can't remember what movie it was. At five when we came out of the Turnage Theater, he said, "Wanna get a cup of coffee?" And then he reached over and buttoned the top button on my raincoat to keep me from getting soaked.

A cup of coffee! Mama didn't even let me smell coffee. Much less drink it. You'd have thought he was asking did I want a bottle of beer, the guilt I suddenly felt. But I said, "Sure."

We sat in back of Morton's Café. Drank coffee, which about gagged me until I learned it needed both cream and sugar. We listened to "Blue Velvet" being sung on the jukebox. And I found out enough about Nicholas Canton to set me on a path I'd not leave easily.

"See," he said, setting his coffee mug on a napkin, careful so it didn't spill from its fullness, "I figure if I work construction a total of seven or eight full weeks out of the summer's twelve, I'll save enough beyond car insurance and gas to pay for extra living expenses next year. I'm on scholarship up in Raleigh at N.C. State. Football scholarship. But they won't let you work during the school year and you gotta have living money. You know?" He hunched his shoulders to say *that's life*.

I nodded. Like I knew! I suddenly wondered what Evelyn Sue did for living money, bedded down on a sleeping bag probably six blocks from Metro Goldwyn Mayer movie studios. She hadn't mentioned it.

"They feed you, don't they?" I looked up at him to see did he have to pay for that, too. I had no notion of what *scholarship* entailed.

"Oh, yeah. But you know, you just hanker for a hamburger or something different . . . food's okay. Not wonderful. Okay."

The silences that came this time were not uncomfortable. Maybe he believed I was a thoughtful person. And I was coming to think he was, too. Not a leave-the-skin-of-your-tires-in-the-street kind of guy after all.

I tried to keep my poise, but I was balancing on a thin

line, because my heart pounded hard. Nicholas Canton was growing. Right in front of my face. He probably was the most beautiful boy I'd ever laid eyes on. Never mind what my first impression had been. It wasn't taking me long to switch that right around. I think it was his smile. When he grinned, he pulled his mouth in a pucker a little at first, like he was holding the smile in, and always, always glanced away. That's what made him come off looking shy. And the way girls looked at him, followed him with their eyes. I noticed that, too.

"I see you got one of them gardenias pinned in your hair," he said, nodding toward the side it was on.

"Yep. Why'd you call it a gardenia? Everybody in these parts calls it a Cape jasmine."

He smiled. Looked at his coffee mug and said, "I'm not *from* these parts." Then looked up to find my eyes.

I wondered what he was doing looking at a Southern girl that way. Wouldn't he rather have a Yankee girl setting here directly across from him? Feisty and strong? Us Southern girls had a reputation for backing down and bending. About as spineless as an amoeba. I know I thought of myself that way when it got down to pure, brick-bottom honesty.

We sat for a minute and then he moved his hand across the table to cup over mine. "When can I see you again?"

I watched his Adam's apple move up and down with the deepness of his voice. Then I hunched I didn't know.

"Your parents?"

He knew. Well I wouldn't tell him the *not our kind of people* part. I just said too old.

"But you're . . . man!" He glanced at the jukebox to collect his thoughts. Then back to me in earnest. "Sometimes folks don't give a person credit for being mature. Here you are. A mature-for-your-age young woman, and yet your parents can't get beyond the fact that they helped you take your first steps, say your first words. In their eyes you'll always be a baby. I know. I fight it every day at my house, too."

"That doesn't mean," I said, being careful of my English so I'd sound as mature as he thought I was, "that I can't see you, Nicholas. We'll just have to meet like this . . ."

Nicholas shook his head. "I don't like doing that. This. We ought to face it head-on and talk it out with them."

"Ha!" I popped in. "You don't know my parents. They don't talk so easy. Not with recent events." Then I told him all about Evelyn Sue.

Before I finished on Evelyn Sue, our own fate had already been decided for us. Miss Wing, our next-door neighbor, came into Morton's from the rain for supper and she saw me sitting at that back table with Nicholas. I told him Mama would know within twenty-four hours.

"How do you know that?"

"Nicholas, you haven't lived in a little town long enough if you don't know that," I told him.

"Who the hell is she, anyway, messing in other people's affairs?" He turned around to take a look at her.

"Evelyn Sue used to tell me Miss Wing's mama, *Mrs.* Wing, was wonderful. Minded her own business, sewed little toys for the kids, passed out candy if you rang her doorbell, Halloween or not. Then she died and *Miss* Wing never married and got sour as a persimmon." I sipped my coffee. "You know what puzzles me?"

He shook his head.

"How come people in families are so different? Here old Mrs. Wing was so wonderful that after she died, the kids all took picnics up to the cemetery and ate on her grave and remembered all the good things about her. And along comes her daughter like the wrath of God . . ."

Nicholas snickered. "Welcome, you have a really unique way of telling things. I could sit all day and listen to you talk."

And so to accommodate him, I said, "You know what I wish?"

He shook his head no.

"I wish that if I die people would picnic right over top of me like Old Mrs. Wing . . ."

"If?"

I thought it over. "Well, *when* then."

And I was right. Not about dying, but about the not even twenty-four hours. The grapevine express runs right to your door if it involves you. That is the rule.

7

"If a small bird falls from its nest," Daddy was saying to me and Nicholas and Mama behind the closed pocket doors of the living room, doors that when open were hidden in the wall, "the parent instinctively will try to save that bird any way it can."

He stopped pacing and talking and looked over at me and Nicholas sitting side by side on the sofa. It had been at my daddy's invitation that Nicholas was sitting there in the first place. Daddy was trying to control the situation from the get-go. Put a stop to it before it began.

"Do you understand the point I'm trying to make, Welcome? By nature, parents want to help their children. This is nothing against Nicholas . . ."

"We haven't done anything wrong," I interrupted this soliloquy on birds. Bees will be next. Who wants to hear sex discussed in front of a boyfriend?

"I'm not saying you have." He sounded testy.

Nicholas didn't say a word. Just sat and listened till my daddy ran out of things to say. I guessed he knew his time would come if he sat long and quiet enough.

"Now . . . you're gonna be a junior come fall, Welcome. In two more years, when you've graduated high school, there will be nothing in the world wrong with you dating a college boy, providing he's upright and decent. But until then I cannot, absolutely cannot, allow it." Daddy was turned, facing the two of us, one hand jingling spare change deep in his pants pocket.

Had I known by how slender a thread my daddy was hanging I might have pushed him. But he sounded in control. Final.

"So, Nicholas," he said. Nicholas never moved a muscle. He was stone. "Have I made my point? Have I made myself clear?"

Nicholas took his time. Didn't jump to the answer. Finally he said, "You have, sir."

Daddy turned and walked to Mama's mahogany secretary where she wrote out checks and balanced the books. I supposed you could call it the financial hub of the house. Money flowed back and forth across her folded-down desk regularly. But it was shut tight now. Like Mama. Even the glass front doors with their diamond-shaped panes were blank and dark, giving no hint of the books she treasured lined up in rows on each shelf. Blank as Mama's eyes. She hated confrontations the way river fish despise hooks that bring them to the surface and out where they can't breathe.

The quiet blew around the room, saving itself for when it would fight to regain control. Because, just as calm as quiet, Nicholas began to say things to my daddy that pierced him.

"I understand your concern, sir. Your not wanting Welcome to become involved with someone older . . ."

"Good then. We are in agreement and there's no need for further discussion . . ."

"If," Nicholas continued as though my daddy hadn't butted in like that, "Welcome doesn't want to see me, then she needs to say so now. Because I will get up and leave and she'll never see me again. Is that what *you* want, Welcome?"

I shook my head.

"Now see here," my daddy roared, "what Welcome wants is of no consequence here. She is not old enough to understand . . ."

"That's not fair . . ." I blurted, but Nicholas was tired of listening and figured the only way he was going to get anything said was to stand his ground. He leaned forward, butted right in, and told my daddy in no uncertain terms that he was willing to stick up for what he believed in and there had to be some rules for debate. He did it this way:

"Excuse me, Mr. O'Neal, but I have listened to what you had to say. Listened respectfully. And now I ask the same consideration from you." He paused long enough to let that sink in. Then he stood and walked to the fireplace, looked at Mama's domed clock sitting there rotating time right on by. When he turned there was a set to his jaw that said he'd thought the situation through and here's what:

"I feel we can reach a compromise. I hear what you're saying. Don't blame you one bit. But suppose Welcome and I see each other under controlled circumstances. Say only at your house or if the four of us should go somewhere together . . ."

My daddy shifted fast and I knew he'd 'bout bit his tongue in two to keep from saying, "In a pig's eye!" But Nicholas went right on like the ripple hadn't occurred.

"Maybe on Sunday mornings I could come over and go to church with your family?"

It was a question, but my daddy probably wasn't trusting his lips to part lest steam come spouting out. Nicholas waited for an answer and when none came, he said, "Surely to God you don't think I'm gonna take advantage of anybody in church!" Said it like he was beginning to feel the strain. Told my daddy with the tone of his voice that he could get mad, too. Was capable of it. And would.

Finally Mama spoke up. Said it seemed a good plan to her. Since Mama was raised by a preacher, she was always on the lookout for souls to save. It was her nature. I could see the missionary wheels turning now. She'd talk to Daddy about it later. For now, Nicholas had the floor and by his tone of voice I knew he was so sure of himself that Daddy would have to scramble around fast for new arguments if he wanted to stay with his convictions.

The upshot of it was that Nicholas got all he asked for. We would be destined to spend our time together that summer in the porch swing. There was no TV at our house, so it was going to have to be the crowded living room, the porch swing, or the back yard garden. And, of course, Sunday mornings at church. And my daddy, who'd sounded like he was in possession of a big, thick rope, turned out he couldn't even hang on to one skinny thread. When Nicholas brought the Lord into it, Daddy's authority snapped like frayed cotton. And somehow that marked the beginning of really bad blood between me and my daddy.

I'd thought with my singing the baccalaureate solo I was on an upswing with Daddy. That and Evelyn Sue taking off the way she did made me look kind of good. But that old you-can-do-better-than-this attitude seeped back in between us. Vinegary and sharp. I felt it every time Daddy and I were in the same room. I'd never be able to please him. So I concentrated on pleasing Nicholas.

Setting in a swing, talking, you find out a lot about a person. I learned that Nicholas wanted to be a lawyer. I'd thought maybe a football coach, but he had different ambitions. And he learned that I had some. Different, too.

"So . . . do you know what *you* wanna do?" he asked me one evening.

"Well, yes. I might like to be a doctor. A pediatrician. Take care of babies."

It was something I thought about from time to time but with no consuming fire of earnestness. Probably wouldn't happen. I'd struggled with chemistry and probably wouldn't be smart enough to cut the mustard. When I'd brought home a C minus in chemistry, Julian had made an offhand remark to Daddy that I held like a night-light in the dark of my mind. Sounded compassionate but, at the same time, less than hopeful. He'd said in a low voice, "Don't be so hard on her, Dad. Girls don't always take to chemistry."

"Why'd she take it in the first place?" Daddy'd asked Julian like I wasn't sitting right there at the dining table with them.

Julian had shrugged. "High hopes, I guess," he'd said for me.

And the message I got from all that was, because I'd been born a girl, it'd be awfully odd if chemistry would be something I could master. It was sort of beyond me.

"Don't you want to stay home and take care of your own children?" Nicholas asked. I shook my head. "That way you'd touch the lives right at your feet." He was already practicing persuasiveness. A good lawyer trait.

I thought about it. "I suppose I could," I said. "But I could do something else as well."

"And let the man make all the money." Nicholas didn't even hear that last part I'd said. Or pay attention to it. He almost sounded like he'd be disappointed in me if I didn't agree with his theory.

I shrugged.

"It'd save money on child care and a maid," he said.

51

"My mama did it, and sewed on the side." Then he leaned back and smiled at me like his mama's doing it was as big as an endorsement from Congress.

We swung in silence a bit. Finally he said, "A man'd be prouder of a wife who worked in the home, a housekeeper."

"Maybe so," I said, folding under that doctor dream to please him. "But it isn't being a *housekeeper*, Nicholas," I added in defense of moms like mine who had stayed at home. "It's a *homemaker*. There's a world of difference. You run the show. You have to be efficient, creative, willing to work hard . . ." If I was going to be a stay-home mom, at least I'd do it right. Give it my best shot.

Nicholas just swung and nodded . . . thinking I'd bought his future for me. And maybe, since it keened so closely with Julian's image of me, maybe I believed it was best.

At church the next Sunday I thought Miss Wing was going to drop her hymnal when she saw us walking in with Nicholas. I glanced over at her and she looked away, losing steam by the minute.

While Nicholas waited for me to file into the row, he shook his arms out straight down to his sides and twisted them so his cuffs would show beyond his coat sleeves. Like he wore a sports jacket every day of the week. Then he took his place beside me on the church pew, followed by Grammie and my parents. And, true to his word, he behaved himself. Sang hymns. Even held the hymnal for me.

During the sermon Grammie went to sleep and sort of slumped against his shoulder. Nicholas grinned over at me and winked. Loved my grandmother to pieces. Enjoyed teasing her when he came to our house. Bugged her about how old she was. When she told him a hundred and three just to shut him up, he'd say, "Well I'll tell you one thing. You've sure got the best-looking hundred-and-three-year-old legs I've ever seen." She'd swat him with whatever she had handy but loved it all the same.

After church, Mama invited Nicholas to Sunday dinner to discuss the sermon. All the while he and Mama batted around ideas and ate fried chicken, Daddy sat silent, knowing full well he'd lost a battle that he'd deemed important.

8

FOURTH OF JULY WEEKEND WE TOOK GRAMMIE TO Virginia Beach to begin a half year visit with Mama's sister, Lacey, and her husband, Mac Hall. Since Evelyn Sue wasn't around, there was extra room in the car, so Trudy rode with us and, after we got there, I broke down and told her about Evelyn Sue leaving in search of James Dean. She vowed she'd never tell it. To anybody.

Then she pumped me for all she was worth about Nicholas Canton. Had he kissed me? Were we going steady? I didn't budge an inch. "I don't make it a habit," I told her, "to discuss the intimate details of my life."

"You always have before," she argued.

"I'm older now. And wiser." And I thought I was.

We came back on Tuesday, and that next Friday afternoon, Nicholas and I went to a movie with his brother, Baron, and his date. Mama had given in and said if we double-dated to the movies in the daytime it'd be okay. She had no idea we wouldn't all be sitting together, the four of us. So at some part of the movie that we laughed over, Nicholas turned toward me, and when the laugh was gone, he leaned in to kiss me. Right there in the movie theater balcony. In a perfect state of confusion I quickly turned back so all he kissed was the side of my face.

Then I ducked my head in embarrassment. Here's what you dream of happening and Lord help you if you don't go and botch the whole thing. But Nicholas could right any wrong. He gentle-like cupped my chin and turned me back and watched my mouth the whole way in for the kiss.

There are people who say—I've heard them—that what you dream about couldn't possibly measure up when it actually happens. I'm here to declare them wrong. When Nicholas, construction worker tan against his white oxford cloth shirt, leaned in to kiss me, Holy Sweet Jesus! I thought I might just slide on through the seat.

Part of the way through the kiss, I opened my eyes to look and, in the flickering light of the movie, I saw his eyebrows all frowned up like he'd been yearning to kiss me as much as I had been wanting him to.

And it did things to my insides, kissing this boy did. No feelings of this kind ever rose in me when Randy Newsome had kissed me on prom night. This was sky high from that first kiss. And it must have moved him too because when he pulled back, his mouth trembled and he tried to smile beyond the tremble, but I saw it and knew.

The movie we saw that day was about a summer in the life of a small-town girl who fell in love with a new guy in town whom her family and most of the town disliked. I lived inside that story because, as I thought about it, I realized it was *my* story. Well, no townspeople had openly come out against Nicholas Canton, except maybe Miss Wing telling Mama she saw me with him in the café. And that was a tossup about whether it was for my own good or against Nicholas. Now Daddy hadn't really cottoned to him, and Mama had said at first that he wasn't our kind of people. Made it sound like he was one of those people living down on Fourth Street. But then Mama had started acting like she accepted him since he'd begun going to church with us every Sunday morning.

I'll admit, sometimes he'd go dark on me. Look so intense and apart. I wasn't sure if he was still with me those times. But more often than not I felt united with him.

At the end of the movie, the girl bucked them all. The whole town. She left everything to go be with the guy the town hated. Trouble was, it didn't show what happened then. The movie ended and you were left holding the bag, hoping it all worked out for her.

Mama was all the time saying love wasn't enough. "Oh, it's all right and all that," she'd say, snapping out clothes to hang up on the line, her eastern North Carolina accent flattening all her *i*'s. I'd hand her a shirt and she'd slide down toward me a step. It was a crab dance in slow motion, and we did it every summer Monday in our back yard. A dance accompanied by Mama's repetitious sermon on love and marriage. "Mind you, love's important but it can't pay the bills. Buy the groceries. Love burns down to embers soon enough."

I'd like to challenge that, I thought, but kept my peace. It would be a no-win argument.

There was no way our love could settle down. It was building day by day. Came a Sunday in August when it was our last night together, since Nicholas had to go off to Raleigh to practice football for N.C. State College the next day. We'd caught lightning bugs in a jar out back. Being kids again. I'd chased one over behind the tool shed and Nicholas hopped a flower bed and landed right next to me. So close, fire nearly ignited.

He pressed my shoulders with both his hands gentle against the rough shed wall and looked at my face for a full minute before he leaned down to kiss me. First said, "I love you with all my heart, girl."

And the kiss itself was one of those long kisses that turned me inside out. Made me want to leave home with its hanging out clothes to dry and ironing pillowcases and handkerchiefs and washing dishes. Made me want to leave all of that. Hop a train. Set up house in a place as small as the tool shed I was pressed up against and prove Mama wrong. Show her that love was enough after all. Just this once. This exception.

9

SEPTEMBER THIRTIETH, I HEARD IT ON THE CAR RADIO when Mama picked me up from the library that evening. James Dean had died. Crashed his Spider Porsche. I wasn't sure Mama and Daddy knew why Evelyn Sue had left for California, only that she'd left. But I knew.

"Welcome, how's your homework . . ."

"Sh-h-h," I hissed, turning up the car radio volume.

". . . died instantly. Dean, a teenage idol, was twenty-four years of age. A memorial service will be held . . ."

Now what? I thought. *What about Evelyn Sue?*

I went straight upstairs, dug out the address she'd sent me in her one and only letter, and wrote her.

> *Dear Evelyn Sue,*
> *I heard about James Dean. I don't know what*

to say. When you left, I didn't understand about loving somebody enough to go in search of them, but now I do.

Write me.

Welcome

Mailed it the next afternoon.

10

Over late summer the iron-strict rule of only porch dating and afternoon matinees had gradually bent and we'd gone to the Cantons' for supper often. So I figured my parents would let me go to a square dance with Nicholas if his parents were going. I was right. Since mid-August he'd been in Raleigh, about six weeks now, for football practice and two games. On one of his twice-weekly telephone calls he told me, because of an open slot in the football schedule, he was coming home this early October weekend. It'd probably be the last weekend we'd be together until Thanksgiving. And we'd already been apart most of the six weeks. He had managed to sneak home overnight twice.

"Now don't you look pretty in your crinolines," Mama said when I came down the stairs to go to the square dance, four crinoline petticoats pushing my skirt out wide. "You've got the prettiest legs, Welcome." Mama's compliments came often these days. I reasoned she felt each compliment was one more payment on an insurance policy she was taking out to keep me from pulling an Evelyn Sue on her and Daddy.

My daddy was conspicuously absent, playing golf on a late Friday afternoon, and I was relieved he wasn't there to frown at Nicholas. And at me for choosing Nicholas.

We went in two cars, mainly because my crinolines took up the entire passenger side of the front seat and then some, and there wouldn't have been room for Mr. and Mrs. Canton and Nicholas's brother. But also, more importantly, we needed two cars so Nicholas and I could have a little kissing time together later.

Dance music was thumping out the open doors of the armory, which I'd always heard was the square dance place to be the first Friday night of every month. I'd never been before, though. People were milling around in the parking lot and, through the open doors, I saw colors whirling past, rotating around that cavern of a room. Made me dizzy from this far. God, please help me when I plunged right into the middle of it.

But we went on in and several people spoke to Nicholas, mostly females, one with wild red hair and a little too much alcohol in her. She grabbed Nicholas by his collar and pulled him close and whispered in his ear. He grinned after taking in what she'd said. Never did volunteer to tell me what she'd told him. She was a little older than I was. What I'd call a real woman.

I didn't know much about square dancing, but Nicholas stuck with me for a while, as much as he could. In square dancing you're always leaving your partner and whirling into another partner's arms. When I'd pass Nicholas on the fly, he'd wink and grin a little without looking straight at me. Feigning that he didn't know me. Smiled just enough so it was like a secret he'd passed on to me. Caused a clutching in my abdomen that made me weak-kneed with passion, I guess. I believed I was sick in love with this boy the ladies all called *Nick*. He'd always be *Nicholas* to me.

About ten minutes into the dance I whirled right into Mr. Canton's arms. "Well, lookee here," he said. It always did seem to me that Mr. Canton appeared amused, like somebody'd just told him a joke and he was still fused with the fun of it. He grinned at me as we do-si-doed, then promenaded around.

"Where's your boy?" he hollered above the music and the amplified voice of the caller.

"Somewhere," I shouted back.

But when we were supposed to reconnect with our partners, Nicholas was nowhere to be seen. I tried to locate him. I wouldn't be honest if I didn't say I thought about that redheaded girl who'd pitched some kind of reel into his ear. Looked like what my mama called a gold digger.

After anything she could get. So I went to the wide-open door and looked outside. Never counted on seeing what I did. I backed up against the cold stone of the building to watch it, too.

A circle of men lounged around in between two cars. Maybe five or six guys. Nicholas, too. And right smack in the middle stood the girl. Made me so mad I wanted to run over there and grab her red hair and yank it out by the roots. There they were passing a whiskey bottle, it looked like. Swigging and passing. I didn't hear all they said. Just an occasional word. Mostly curse words. Nicholas was right there swigging and passing, too. And laughing. A lot of laughing.

I watched a full five minutes I know, and would probably have continued to do so for lack of courage, had it not been for this oily person who came and stood next to me like I'd offered my company. I shot a real sideways glance, not turning my head.

"What's a sweetheart like you doing standing out a dance?" he asked, and I smelled the liquor on his breath, a green smell that burned my nostrils like peppermint.

I didn't look at him. Just said carefully, "Waiting for somebody."

"Will I do?" he asked.

Oh, Lord. You wouldn't do if you turned out to be the only man left in North America, I wanted to say but just didn't answer. Another sideways glance showed black hair shining with too much Vitalis. Thick and plastered. He had the lean look of a coyote. And underneath the hair, slanting, squinty, shifty eyes.

Now, truth be known, if I'd been able to see ahead, I would have taken him up on it. Whatever *it* was. I would have danced with that man and hunted for Mr. Canton, then asked him to take me home. Or called my daddy.

But instead, I left Mr. Coyote leaning on air up next to the wall and I walked out to the circle of men and one girl. Right on up to Nicholas Canton like I owned him, which I thought I did.

"I wondered where you went," I said, firm.

He blinked. Surprised to see me, though I'd be hard pressed to know what he thought I'd be doing by myself back there in an armory full of strangers.

"Here I am," he said, squinting at me because the parking lot light was directly at my back and in his eyes.

"Can we go on in?" I asked next.

He thought about it. Finally shook his head. I couldn't tell if he was out-and-out drunk, but I knew he was sure feeling his liquor.

"Let's cut out," he said to me. "See you guys."

"Hm-m-m-m-uh!" one of them hummed as we walked off. "M-m-m-m-m-m-m!" another sealed the silence like he'd just tasted something delicious.

I followed Nicholas to his car and he climbed right in. Clean forgot about me standing over by the passenger door. Didn't have the first thought about opening my door for me the way he'd taken to doing after that first ride together.

When he started the engine, I figured I'd better hop on in before I got left high and dry.

"Should you be drivin'?" I asked.

"I'm not drunk," he said defensively. "I know what I'm doing." So I let it alone. Sat way over from him. Should have said, *Take me home.*

Not wobbly, but he did drive slow, like he was hunting something.

"Checking for deer?" I asked once. He and his brother hunted deer together every Christmas break. But he shook his head.

We rode on past the outskirts of Lily, houses sparser and sparser. Little lit rectangles, boxes of lights, set way back from the road. Finally he slowed and turned down a dirt road toward the river.

"Where're we going?" I asked, sitting forward to see in the dark, nervous and madder than a bee-stung baby.

Nicholas didn't answer and I checked him often to see was he still awake. His eyes were open but he was right glassy-eyed.

Finally he pulled off the dirt road into a lane that extended about a quarter of a mile up a hill. Turned out it was a driveway to a dark-windowed house. Nicholas pulled into the yard, then backed around, facing the road down below and the river out beyond. I could see houses on the other bank, high above their boat piers. He turned off the lights, and the black hole of Calcutta my grammie was always bringing up couldn't have been any blacker. I was glad when the moon slid out from behind a cloud so I could see his face. He was smiling.

"What's up, sweetcakes?" Nicholas whispered, grinning.

I just blinked so I could see him better. There I sat, wreathed by my stiff crinolines and not knowing what would come next.

"Say something," he whispered.

What I wanted to say was, *Who are you?* This was not the Nicholas Canton I'd known all summer.

He hiccupped and grinned. Slid down and leaned his head on the back of the car seat.

We just sat. I wasn't sure what to do. I'd never been in the wilderness with a boy by myself before. And was I mad!

"A boy doesn't just take a girl to a dance and up and leave her on her own," I said, looking straight ahead at the windshield.

Nicholas shifted. "Darlin'," he said, and the word was like a foreign language, the way he said it to me. "Darlin', we're done dancin'. Here we sit, and kissing's not all I got in mind tonight." I looked over at him in time to see him smile again and then pass out cold.

Well! Don't that take the cake, I thought. *Here we set in the middle of nowhere and he's out like a light.*

Took me a little to calm down, but I finally did figure out what to do. I got out. Pulled and dragged Nicholas over to the passenger side. He never even woke up. Then me and my crinolines climbed behind the wheel.

Now my daddy'd been letting me drive in the church parking lot some evenings, so I did know about a clutch. How it can buck you if you don't ease and gun just right.

We didn't buck too much. Came down onto the dirt road. Turned back toward town and drove right on in past the Gulf station, turned at Jay Hue's Cleaners and cruised down Market, taking a left on Main.

I parked Nicholas's car right in front of his house. Thought hard about what to do next. Then decided. Left him passed out in the passenger seat. He'd have to explain to his mother and daddy how their football hero son got back from the dance.

Then I marched right up the middle of the street, heading west. Heading home. Afraid of the dark sidewalks.

I never did tell Mama. Might have if Evelyn Sue hadn't chosen that night to show up from California, traveling lighter but wiser. Julian and Wysteria had come over and everybody seemed genuinely glad to see her. At least by the time I got there.

"Welcome," Evelyn Sue said after the house had settled down. Julian and Wysteria had left, and Mama and Daddy were in their bedroom, probably whispering away about this sudden turn of events. Evelyn Sue and I were sitting in our pajamas on the dark front porch, receiving the strong, salty smell of the river and listening to the small-town stillness that leaks in after midnight. "Welcome, it's good to be home."

"How'd Mama and Daddy take it when you showed up?" I looked over to ask her.

She laughed. "They were on the porch when Sandy drove me up. Daddy was hid behind the evening paper, but Mama . . . she stood up and walked slow to the top of the porch steps. Just stood there and watched me coming up the front walk."

She stopped and I could tell by her voice she had taken a sudden plunge because what she said next was filtered through trying not to cry. "When she saw it was me, she lit out down the steps and said, 'Here . . . let me help you carry your stuff, Evelyn Sue.' Not where you been or do you know how much you hurt me by up and leaving, but, *Here, let me help you carry your stuff.*"

After a minute I said, "And Daddy?"

She shrugged. "You know Daddy. He growled a while but when he hugged me I knew I was back in. He did say I'd need to go to school or work, one. Wasn't going to put up with my lying around the house."

"What school?" I asked her. She'd finished her freshman year at East Carolina Teachers' College just twenty-two miles away. "E.C.T.C.?"

But she shook her head. "No." Here she paused and found her own dream I guess, her present dream in the light of California hard-times living. "I think, for now, I'd like to go to beauty school. Nothing really challenging.

Because as soon as I meet the right man, no longer Mr. Perfect, but just a guy I can love, well, we'll marry and I'll stay home and have babies. You know?"

I nodded. Sat there on the porch in the October chill that comes past sundown and is hard present by midnight, sat there and understood exactly. It was what was expected of girls. We were raised watching our mothers as they made everything turn out right. Do-gooders. It was a way of thinking I guessed I was going to have to buy into if I was going to stick with Nicholas. Wasn't all too sure I was in a sticking mood.

Evelyn Sue sat a long while and then cleared her throat and said, "Welcome, sometimes it doesn't quite do you to follow your heart."

She'd said it so low I could barely hear her. I just sat applying that to me.

"But you do find, finally," she went on, "the only person you can trust is yourself. You might have to back up and go down a different road to find out. And that takes a big person to be able to do that."

So, what? What did she mean? Had she already given up on finding James Dean even before he died? Did she still love him? Did she start home as soon as she heard? I wouldn't have said it for real money, but she'd stood as much chance of finding him back in June as she did now. Zero.

But for now that was all she said. It was something I really needed to hear this night, though. I took her words in and mulled them over. Knew I needed to make them mine. *The only person you can trust is yourself.* I watched clouds slide over the moon like it was gone for the night. Then suddenly it'd take the edge of a cloud where it was thin and glow right through it and pop out from behind like it was reborn. Watching the moon birth itself over and over should have pushed me into a mood for changes, too. But I guess I wasn't ready yet.

II

Everybody knows late summer in the South is akin to hell and October isn't that much better. Rose gardens are still blooming hot pink and white and red. Being fall in name only didn't offer a lot of relief. Dog days with hot daytimes and cool nights. The humidity still soaking its wet heat up under your bangs, making for thin trickles of salty sweat along about fifth period at school, wiping out Revlon's Touch and Glow makeup as it slid. Add to this the elastic tension of a boyfriend who suddenly no longer spoke to you. He'd always phoned Monday and Thursday nights from college. No more.

Then add a sister who'd just returned after a summer in search of a hero who died right under her nose, in a manner of speaking. Evelyn Sue whined and griped about the humidity, no dates. You'd think she'd forgotten how glad she'd sounded to be home that first night. But the silent

71

telephone was for her as well as for me. Though I didn't voice it the way Evelyn Sue did, its very silence found home base in the deepest part of me.

I wanted to climb to the rafters in the ancient tool house that stood in our back yard, snatch down the hornets' nest with my bare hands, and let them eat me alive. Fill me with their venom and be quick about it. So when I fell off the stepladder, I'd be too undone to tell which end was up and I'd break my neck. It'd be short and violent enough to make Nicholas Canton sorry he'd ever toyed with my heart. It was elaborate, and I dreamed about it in my spare time. I sat at my open windows early evenings, feeling for the slightest hint of an autumn breeze, and slowly, increasingly, I began to believe my life was over.

I was mad at Nicholas. Mad as hops. But I also still loved him. He, on the other hand, should have been asking, no, *begging* for my forgiveness. But the tables were turned and it appeared he didn't even care to speak to me. Didn't call, write, much less offer to drive to Lily and come over. *Maybe,* I reasoned, *he's figured I'm too much woman for him. Got a mind of my own, wanting to be a doctor.* It helped my feelings to believe that, whether or not it was true. Maybe he figured I was trouble. Plain old hard-luck trouble.

I guessed telling Evelyn Sue was out of the question. She appeared too absorbed in restarting her own life in Lily. I couldn't even tell Trudy about it, though she asked. Came by every day or so after school. Truth be known, I was ashamed Nicholas wasn't mine anymore to brag about.

And then, too, Trudy hadn't kept her word before. Had spilled the beans about Evelyn Sue and now half the high school kept asking me daily if my sister was over James Dean yet since he'd up and died.

"How'd you find out?" I finally asked Darlene Brigman.

"Trudy Hampton," she said, and I knew not to trust Trudy ever again.

Finally one evening, when Evelyn Sue came in to borrow my half slip, she asked, "What's eating you, Welcome?" She had a date with a boy she'd graduated with and I was so relieved for her that she'd found somebody that a small part of me felt happy. But large parts remained aching and cold. For myself. "Have you been moping these four solid months, ever since I've been gone?"

I shook my head.

She came over and sat on the carpet beside me. "Then what, Wel?"

It seemed suddenly that she really did care. Had stepped outside her own problems long enough to see the muddle I was in. So I spilled all of it. She sat, thought awhile, and surprised me. I'd thought she'd say up front what a fool I was for mooning over a boy who'd blown it. Who owed me an extreme apology.

"Welcome, you are a wonderful person." I shook my head I wasn't. "Don't you have any self-esteem?" she finally asked.

"Guess not," I said, looking at my ugly feet. My ugly legs. My hair, limp with perspiration.

73

"Well, first off, you need a do-over."

I just sat. Whatever a do-over was, it wouldn't be enough.

"We need to cut your hair. Give you a perm. Lie out in the sun for hours, Wel. After that we'll see what else you need to get you back on track. I'll help you tomorrow. You'll see. Just doing something, taking the first step, will jerk you right out of the doldrums."

She snatched the half slip out of my bureau drawer and was gone. I watched from the window as she and her date left in his car. Somehow the whole Evelyn Sue moment hadn't helped a thing.

She meant what she'd said, though. The next day was Saturday, and she had time off from the beauty parlor where she was in training. She trained some more on me, I guess. Whacked my hair from nearly my waist all the way to my shoulders. And permed a gentle curl all through it. But first we lay in the back yard on white sheets and baked ourselves brown, smearing baby oil laced with iodine over every part of our bodies that showed.

Over at the high school six blocks away we could hear snatches of the band practicing. Its horns and drums coming across the hot October air in the form of odd notes of music and rhythm. Sounded like the pulse of Lily, for the moment, telling me that the heart of the town was still beating whether I was part of its life or not. Throbbing away time. Pulling winter closer by the beat.

Evelyn Sue and I talked about her California experience.

"So, when'd you decide to come back?" I asked her. Had

in mind *the very day he died* or *when I realized a week later there was nothing to stay for.*

But she took a while to answer and then all she said was, "I didn't belong."

I squinted at her and shaded my eyes so I could see her better.

"I really did love James Dean," she said at last. "Do." She smoothed oil on her legs. "Loving a person you actually know as opposed to somebody you've never met is what we're supposed to do, though. I figured out that much."

"Why?" Seemed to me carrying a torch for somebody who couldn't hurt you wouldn't be too bad, after all. And I said so.

"True," Evelyn Sue said and flipped over on her stomach. "But then he can't help you either."

"Help you?"

She nodded. "I think, now don't hold me to this, but from watching the people I know, my friends, I think not only is it a miracle when two people love each other, but if it's strong enough, you both probably grow up because of it." And then she propped herself up on her elbows and told me about this couple she met in L.A. "Been together five years," she said, "and are more in love now than at the start; at least that's what they said. They treated each other like friends, not husband and wife. You know what I mean?"

I nodded. I guessed I knew.

Mama leaned out the back porch door to shake the dust

mop. "You girls don't get burned, you heah? You can't go missing church tomorrow now on account of sunburn."

That was just like Mama. Planning her life around church on Sundays. God forbid you should ever miss church. Her sharp eyes would shave off any excuse you would try to invent.

When Mama went in I asked, "Do you think Mama and Daddy ever felt that way?"

Evelyn Sue shrugged then shook her head. "Not now anyway. I don't think they even *see* each other anymore. Like your right arm. It's there every day, does all the stuff it's supposed to. But do you ever thank it?"

"It's part of your body," I said in defense of right arms.

"Exactly," Evelyn Sue said and turned away to put a period at the end of this conversation. I looked at her back broiling in the sun and wondered what gave her the right to so much wisdom. How'd I know it was true? Maybe every marriage became flat and even and boring.

I lay down beside her and thought about Mama and Daddy and pictures I'd seen when they first got married and the look in Mama's eyes when she was staring up at Daddy in those pictures. And wondered why the look went away.

12

Surely there is a statute of limitations on mad, I thought along about late October. *Nicholas can't stay mad forever.* I was pretty much past my anger. Why wasn't he? For him to be this mad, his mama must have really come down on him hard for being parked out in front of the house, dead drunk.

Meanwhile, up at our end of the street things were really humming along. I had been asked out by several boys but nothing serious. Mama was so glad to have Evelyn Sue back, she still fried chicken twice a week and cranked out cobblers and cakes like they were letters she was sending in envelopes. Here Evelyn Sue had been home almost a month now and still Julian's family ate dinner with us every chance they got. We even had a cookout down by the riverfront park. That was when Julian dropped his bombshell.

"Welcome, I saw that boy you were seeing."

I looked up. "Nicholas Canton?"

He nodded.

"Where?" Hoped my face didn't betray me and speak of the cold finger that gouged inside me.

"When we were up to Raleigh buying fall clothes for the young'uns. On Fayetteville Street at Ivy Taylor's. He and some long-haired blond girl walked past and headed on into the Ambassador Theater."

"Yeah," I said, licking my fingers from a rack of vinegar barbecue ribs I was working on. "We broke up."

Daddy dropped the spoon in the baked beans when he heard that. I figured happiness jolted right through his body and caused him to jerk. I also figured it was true, our breaking up. But still found myself wondering why and aching for a person I didn't even need to be thinking about. Since a girl wouldn't have been caught dead calling a boy on the telephone, I hadn't. Had thought about it hard, though. I'd have even swapped Daddy any day of the week if he was thinking about letting me back into his favor now. Swapped him for Nicholas in a heartbeat.

Along about Halloween I got a long-distance call on a Tuesday evening. Mama caught it.

"Hell-a. Who? Just . . . just a minute. . . . Welcome, it's for you. Long-distance. Person-to-person . . ."

It was the first person-to-person long-distance phone call I'd ever received and I knew before I got to the phone it must be Nicholas Canton, saying how he'd not been able to get me off his mind. Saying he was sorry. He'd always called station-to-station before, though. Never went through an operator. That in itself should have warned me.

"Hello."

"Is this Miss Welcome O'Neal?" The operator.

"Yes."

"Sir, your party is on the line."

Silence. "Hello," I said again.

"Welcome? This is Randy Newsome . . ."

I turned my back to Mama standing in the hall. Faced the diamond-shaped glass inlays framing the front door with their fractured versions of the streetlight shining through.

Randy wanted me to catch the bus to Raleigh on Saturday morning and go to the N.C. State/Clemson football game that afternoon with him.

"I'd have you back to the bus station by eight that night. I've already checked the bus schedule. You'd get back to Lily by about midnight."

"This Saturday?" I asked.

"Yeah. Is that possible?"

"Can you hold on while I ask my mama?"

"Yeah." His voice sounded thin and tinny through the phone, squeezed by one hundred eighty-two miles of phone lines. "Don't forget this is long-distance, though, so make it quick."

Mama had to ask Daddy. But, truth be known, they were both so glad Nicholas Canton was out of my life, they didn't take long to say yes.

After I'd hung up the phone I slipped out the front door

and stood on the dark porch and looked at the lights moving on the river. Boats with fishermen trolling in the dark October night, hoping for fish to sell tomorrow at the fish markets in town. *Fresh fish,* they'd say. Packed on crushed ice. Staring at you with flat black eyes. Whatever had made them glide through water now gone. That invisible part that fills us all, animals and humans, drained.

Loving somebody is sort of like that, I found myself thinking. *It's invisible. Love could go and you'd feel empty.* What I wondered . . . was it as final as death? Or could it fill you again one day? Take you by surprise, though this time you'd have a name for it? Know it for what it was? And be glad it came again?

13

Randy met me in Raleigh at the Trailways bus station at around noon on Saturday. A strong smell of black exhaust hung in the air, coating the outside of the depot, the newspaper stand, the benches.

"So, how you been?" he asked, then stuck both hands in his pants pockets and rocked in his loafers.

Here's a boon: Randy Newsome had stretched on out that summer he was away until he was nearly as tall as I was! Still had reddish hair, more freckles than ever, and the same chipped tooth, same lopsided grin where the right side shot up higher than the left, and he sort of cocked his head to one side like he was analyzing you while he grinned. But taller, and that was amazing. I wanted to ask him if they fed him fertilizer down at Camp Seagull or how else did he sprout up so.

"How you been?" he asked again when I didn't answer the first time.

"Fine," I lied. What was I to say? Well, my real boyfriend, the one I think about day and night, has ditched me good? Has got some long-haired girl he's seeing now? No. "Just fine."

We walked to his car. I had no luggage to wait for.

At lunch at the S & W Cafeteria down on Fayetteville Street there was a pregnant woman behind us in line. Real pregnant. When we passed the desserts and I was picking up my water glass, she reached the display of pecan and custard and cherry pies. Chocolate layer cake. Coconut cake. She took three of them.

"I think my eyes are bigger than my stomach," she bleated out like a billy goat fixing to munch down on somebody's prize petunias.

I glanced back at Randy, who had turned his head to look at the woman. So we both saw her husband cast a cockeyed look down at her whale belly and mutter, "Impossible." And he said it twice. Not once, but twice. That man was living on the edge. I'd have warped him with my shoulder bag, I'd a been her.

As it was, Randy and I strangled so hard with trying to keep from howling with laughter we almost didn't make it to a table after Randy paid the cashier. He stopped to wipe his eyes with his handkerchief before he unloaded his tray. Just set the tray of food on the table and laughed hard into his white handkerchief. Me, I wasn't carrying one, so I unrolled my silverware and fell apart right in the linen napkin.

So the afternoon started off really fine. We made it to the stadium in time. Randy spoke to lots of people, and I figured, by the time he was a senior, he'd be president of the student body again. We were soaking up the sun and the crowd and the popcorn and peanut hawkers when the loudspeaker system came alive.

"Welcome to today's game between the Tigers of Clemson University and the North Carolina State College Wolfpa-a-a-ck! It's footba-a-a-ll Saturday!"

People screamed like he'd announced the second coming. I was settling on in, basking in the almighty noise that fills a stadium, when the announcer began calling out the starting lineups. Visitors first, the Tigers. The whole team ran onto the field together as he called their names. When he finished with the visitors, the cheerleaders rolled out a great big wheel, standing on its edge. A hoop skinned over with tight red paper. Then the announcer called the North Carolina State offensive starting lineup and out each one jumped through that hoop like eleven trained seals. The first one broke the paper for the rest. One name he called gave me pause.

"At quarterba-a-ack is Edward Gibson from Lebanon, Tennessee. A-a-and at running back, from Lily, North Carolina, is Nicholas Ca-a-a-nton . . ."

A big roar from the crowd and I split right in half. Now, I'd known Nicholas would be playing. Felt I'd be all right with it, though. Never realized how it'd hit me and knock the wind right out of me. Leave me feeling a shell where a flash fire had incinerated all in me.

Well, I pulled myself back together again. Nicholas Canton wasn't going to mess up my first date to a college football game. But he did. Because he was everywhere. Doing everything. I welcomed halftime so it'd be a relief from hearing that boy's name. And, in the second half, I watched his helmet dodge and leap and remembered how it felt when he kissed me and the unsure way his mouth trembled when he was done.

When we flowed out of Riddick Stadium with the twenty-three thousand other football fans, I hoped Randy wasn't going to notice how hollow I was. Hoped he'd do most of the talking.

We drove all over Raleigh. Listened to Teresa Brewer bawl out "Til I Waltz Again with You," then Eddie Fisher, "I'm Walking Behind You." Neither of which improved my mood any.

At traffic lights, when we were held up, Randy told me the new "watch-out" jokes that were all the rage.

"Watch out for that clothesline!" he said. Then added the punch line, "What clothes li-ay-ay-ay-ay-yine?"

"Watch out for that hole! What ho-o-o-o-o-ole?"

"Watch out for that golf ball! What golf ba . . . ?"

Trying to be a good sport, I showed him the "Mom,

you've plaited my braids too tight" look. He hadn't seen that.

It was getting dark early, threatening rain. I took off the white mum Randy had pinned to my blouse. "Sure smells good," I told him.

He smiled over at me.

When we turned into Pullen Park, I asked, "Where we going now?"

"I'm gonna show you some ducks and swans down to the lake," and we turned down a small road and parked beside the lake. But the rain had started and the water that should have been smooth got as puckered as chicken flesh, pocked by hard, driving rain.

"Reckon those ducks and swans done took cover," he said and slid his arm around my shoulders.

Now one of the things I'd learned from Nicholas Canton was how to kiss good. No flattened-out balloon kisser with lips sealed shut, not me. So when Randy leaned over to kiss me, I closed my eyes and kissed right back. And somehow with my eyes shut, it was a little like kissing Nicholas. So I did a dangerous thing. Right there in Randy Newsome's roommate's '52 Ford's front seat, I replaced him. I kept my eyes shut to reality and kissed Nicholas with all my might, making up for lost time. Making up in my mind what he would tell me about being mad because his mama raised all kinds of fireworks over him sleeping off a drunk in front of his house.

Randy began kissing in earnest and got what Trudy

called W.H.T. Wandering Hand Trouble. Only it wasn't any trouble to me because he was Nicholas and I welcomed every move he made.

And so, on a stormy Saturday afternoon in late October, Nicholas Canton made some kind of passionate love to me. Everything he did seemed natural and the way I'd imagined it over and over. Of course, it was my very first time, though, and I heard his voice whisper, "You're a virgin, aren't you, Welcome?" And I nodded because I couldn't trust my own voice at that point. "Me, too," he said.

When we were done and the only sound was raindrops on the car top, I kept my eyes shut tight. Smelled Nicholas's aftershave and heard him moving to get straight. Heard him whisper, "Welcome?"

But I didn't want to leave where I was.

"Welcome? Are you all right?"

I nodded.

"Well, open your eyes . . . so I'll know."

I did. But instead of dark hair, there was red. And instead of the trembling smile, there was Randy's lopsided grin with the one chipped tooth in the middle. And instead of my heart, I had given him my body.

14

THANKSGIVING. THAT NOISY, GOOD-SMELLING HOLIDAY when there is no gift-giving, which then equals no hurt feelings. Just stuffing: the turkey, yourself. Amazed at how much food you can put away and still walk. Not just roll over on your side and slide into a coma. And by late November cold weather finally shows up, even as far south as Carolina. And it's welcome. On its frosty air all the cinnamon smells slide along.

Wysteria brought pumpkin pies. Said she'd made twelve. "Little Julian and Mary Walter passed them around all over the neighborhood," she said. Which explained what they were wearing. Little Julian had on black pants with a large cardboard belt buckle wrapped in foil, a navy blue blazer, white shirt, and a Pilgrim hat. For my money he looked for all the world like the penguin from the KOOL cigarette pack. Mary Walter had on one of Wysteria's dark, flowered summer dresses with a wide belt along about the waist of the dress (which hit Mary Walter below the hips). If she was a Pilgrim, I was a gorilla. I was betting their neighbors were still laughing behind their hands, but eating pumpkin pie all the same.

Along about four in the afternoon, when we all began to make sounds like we might be able to hold dessert after all, Mama took a notion that whipped cream wasn't enough. And when Mama got something in her head, it was no use trying to shake her loose from it. "We need vanilla ice cream to go on the mince pie. Whipped cream's too thin. It's all right on pumpkin pie 'cause it's light. But not mince pie."

I knew what Mama meant, too. All that melding of apples and raisins and whole cranberry sauce with pecans and spices and brown sugar and brandy thrown in needed solid cold on top, running down into its core when you cut a forkful.

"I'll go get it," I volunteered. Driving solo was one of my new accomplishments.

"You got keys?" Daddy asked me as I flung my winter coat on and headed for the kitchen door.

"Yessir." I passed Wysteria still washing the good china rimmed in gold and the crystal, which couldn't go into the dishwasher. Might fade the etching right off it.

The only market open on Thanksgiving Day was Scott's, way out the Pactolus Highway. Carl Scott was a bachelor and always made good money being open on holidays.

Must have been worth his while because he never closed on a special day.

At the traffic light coming onto the highway from the outskirts of Lily I pulled up short. It'd been yellow but I decided not to push my luck. Didn't want anything to mar my clean driving record.

I was drumming my fingers on the leather steering wheel cover, waiting for the longest light in the history of mankind, when I heard the small, short tootings of a horn. Looked to my left to see the car that had slid up beside me in the left-hand turn lane.

When I glanced that way, it was the car and not the person I recognized. Black '51 Chevy. Then I looked through the two windows, mine and his, to see Nicholas Canton. He nodded at me. Solemn. I just looked. Didn't react. Just looked.

I felt the light would go green any second, so I was setting up to shift my eyes back to the light when he made his move. Shot his forefinger right at me like a gun. And with the bang of the silent gun his thumb fired off, he mouthed, "I love you." Big and bold.

Good for me. I never batted an eye. I let him know I'd seen, then turned just in time to see the light change green. Gently rolled out of there without even a backwards glance.

And what that does to a person's insides is directly dependent on how much love is left over. In my case, quite a bit. So when I got out of my car at Scott's Market, there was a small volcano erupting somewhere under my skin. Tearing at tissue. Sucking feelings from their buried places.

I went on into Scott's. Picked out the vanilla ice cream. Paid for it. Double sacked it. Headed back outside when who was leaning on my car? Must have U-turned on the Pactolus Highway and hunted me down. Parked right up next to me and was waiting to intercept me like I was a high spiral from a quarterback.

I looked him square in the eye and said, "Please move. My ice cream will melt." Like it wasn't twenty-eight degrees right where we stood. Nothing was going to melt. But I was going to make him work for it before I gave in.

He just stood. Solemn. "Welcome, I miss you."

I'd been looking at his third button down on his sports jacket. Now I shifted up to his face. His green eyes looking from one eye to the other, trying to find me inside.

But a voice deep inside me sent up and out the words, "Tough break." Surprised the heck out of me. Certainly not my voice. Some Yankee girl who'd taken me over and was suddenly driving now.

He blinked. Frowned.

"Now if you'll step aside, I have places to go."

Nicholas reached out then and grabbed my coat sleeve. "Listen to me, Welcome. I was wrong. Wrong to get drunk on you that night. Then wrong not to patch things up. Okay? I know that now." These were the very words I'd waited almost two months to hear him say.

But that Yankee girl I couldn't help but love, who surged me with power, said simply, "It's a bit late. Move." And what she saw was what I saw. Nicholas Canton with a long-haired girl walking along Fayetteville Street up in Raleigh. Going into the Ambassador Theater. There was no forgiving inside me after all.

"You've changed," he finally said, stepping away from my daddy's car. "Where's the Welcome O'Neal I fell in love with?"

I opened the door, threw the sack of ice cream across the seat, got in, slammed the door, put the key in the ignition, turned it on, cut the radio back, rolled down my window. All this before I said the one word that Yankee girl told me I'd better be saying. "Gone."

Then she smiled, right up through me. Used my body that day. Made it tough as everyday china. No longer fragile and etch-wary. Solid and shiny.

I did raise my eyebrows for them to say, *So there. Live with it.* Then backed around and out of Nicholas Canton's life. Knew he was indelibly fastened to a certain summer in me that was gone. As gone as he was.

15

Yep! You bet it can. Lydia Meyers was right. It can happen with just one time. Not even a try. Just a time. Hard to imagine all those people working so hard at making a little bitty baby and, lo and behold, one time's all it takes for some of us.

I pretty much guessed along about the beginning of the first week of December, when I was almost a month late for my period and getting deathly sick every morning. Thank goodness for cold weather and tree leaves turning to announce rain on the way. I'd have died had it been August.

It wasn't easy to accept. I kept hoping no. Cried into my pillow every single night. Considered suicide twice. But after a week and then a second slid by, the blackness of this new reality settled in and was still hard to deal with, but not as hard as the nausea right then. *What am I going to do with a baby?* I thought, hanging over the bathroom sink. *Where can I turn? Stay inside the house when I begin to show? All those months until it is born? And then what? Say we found it on the porch?*

I don't want a baby, I raged inside. Dreamed one night I had fifteen. At one time. Became the first woman in history to have a multiple birth that large. Was asked to bring all fifteen and be interviewed in New York City on the *Today Show.*

"How about feeding time?" Dave Garroway asked me. I'd seen him on TV when we'd stayed with Aunt Lacey in the summer. "How do you manage feeding time?"

"It never stops," I told him, rocking two in my arms and bumping the car porta-bed with two more in it. "It never stops." Even the television crew were pitching in, feeding bottles to hungry ones, diapering wet ones.

In my dream, Mama had been so mortified about my illegitimate birthing feat, she wouldn't even fly to New York with me and my babies. Evelyn Sue had gone instead. Being on national TV hadn't bothered me, though. In my dream, everybody I cared about in Lily already knew. What difference then that people from Texas to Michigan also knew? Maybe somebody'd take pity and send help. Evelyn Sue and I were working our fingers to the bone as it was.

When I woke, I lay on sheets damp with perspiration and grew so nauseated I didn't even try to make it to the bathroom. Heaved right in the sheets. Then lay awake til dawn with my very own primary problem that obliterated any and everything else.

And in all that early morning thinking, never once did it enter my mind that Randy might be a way out. He was no more the father of this child than Jerry Lewis was. Randy may have been the means, but it was my fault, not his. On that rainy October afternoon, Nicholas fathered this unborn child. In my mind. And now not even he could be the father because, replacing the love I had felt for him was beginning a cold hatred. I'd finally recognized him for who he was. He no more cared about me than he did the girl up in Raleigh. I was just another girl. The one back in Lily. Convenient.

"Come on, Welcome," my daddy called up the stairs. "It's seven forty-five and you're gonna be late for school."

I got up off my knees from beside the toilet bowl where I'd spilled my guts. Had thought I was over it but when I'd crawled out of bed, there it had come again.

"Be right there," I called down to him on my way out of the bathroom. My breasts were growing like two cantaloupes. Firm, though, as I took the stairs slow. No bouncing.

I was white as a light bulb, I noticed in the hall mirror before I left. Mama didn't notice, though. Just passed me a sack lunch I'd not eat and said, "Have a good day, hon." Peeling potatoes and scraping carrots for soup was a chore you wouldn't want to look away from lest you took the skin off your forefinger.

Daddy looked. I could count on him. Probably because he cared so much. Was always the one to protect me, even if it was in a blustering way. "You feel bad?" he asked at the stoplight at Second and Market.

I nodded. "Tired," which was the very understatement of the year.

I took in a deep breath and prayed I'd not gag in front of anybody, him most of all. Just wanted to be alone, actually. I was too tired to deal with anything.

Trudy'd kept calling when I wouldn't give her the time of day at school. But I wasn't taking phone calls anymore. Least of all from blabbering Trudy. Would yell out through my closed bedroom door to Mama, "Tell her I'm doing my homework. I'll call her later."

Even when Randy called. Same answer.

But I never did. Never called anybody back.

16

Evelyn Sue came home from a date at midnight on Saturday, December fourteenth. I was waiting up. Lying across her bed so I'd be sure to be awake or wakened.

"Good grief, Welcome! You scared me half to death." She took off her sweater collar. Then her sweater and skirt. "I thought you were a dead body lying there." Her muffled voice from beneath her slip, high over her head, asked in its own way what I was doing there.

But I didn't answer until she was done and in her flannel pajamas, sitting cross-legged at the foot of the bed.

"What's up?" She pulled her necklace chain around in front and, tucking her chin to see, found the clasp and undid it. I didn't say a word until I had her undivided attention. When she looked over at me, I sat up and said, "I'm pregnant."

I just thought I fell apart inside when Evelyn Sue had

spilled her news last summer. This, however, was something that couldn't be easily undone. I couldn't change my mind, come back home, and it'd be gone.

"Skip rope," she said finally, after her unstrung jaw had sealed.

"What?" It was a whisper because I thought she'd gone instantly insane. She looked mad as a mullet. Her eyes bulged. Mouth flopped wide again.

"Skip rope," she said once more.

"What's that got to do with anything?" I asked cautiously. Next she'll say, *Climb a magnolia tree.*

"If you skip rope, it can jar it loose."

"And," I asked after a minute, "what if that doesn't work?"

"Then we'll . . . uh . . . it'll give us some time to think."

What I was getting out of this conversation was a "we" thing, not a "you" feeling. It wasn't me alone in this problem anymore. Evelyn Sue was inside it with me. That helped, so I jumped rope every afternoon after school out in back of the toolshed. Thought about Lydia Meyers. She'd been in ninth grade when her it-only-takes-one-time time came. Out of the clear blue she'd just stopped coming to school. Then, of course, we all heard why: she'd got herself in trouble. I had laughed like everybody else. Now *I* was Lydia Meyers.

Three days of jumping rope didn't jar a thing loose. I reported to Evelyn Sue every night.

"Oh well," she said, "it was worth a try. I was afraid it

wouldn't work. How far along are you?"

"About six weeks. Or seven."

She screwed her face up to think. "Have you told Nicholas?" I blinked and looked at the floor. "Well, you have, haven't you?"

Shaking my head no, I said to the floor, "He's not the father."

"What?" It was a loud whisper that blew Evelyn Sue straight down to the floor where she'd been standing. "Good Lord, Welcome. Who else could it be?"

And that was the very moment I decided. By saying I didn't know, I could keep who the daddy was inside me and silent as this baby. At least until I could make up my mind about telling Randy. He'd have to know first. It would hold until I saw him in person. By then I'd have sorted it out.

"I don't know."

"You what!" I thought she was going to turn inside out, she was so mad. "Well, that's a fine fix. I guess we'll just have to tell Mama and Daddy."

I was afraid of that. "I believe I'd rather run away," I told her.

"Well you can't. You have to stay and face the music." This from the very person who had run off to Hollywood, which I didn't bother to remind her. Then she softened and said she had one more ace up her sleeve. I was hoping it was a luckier plan than jumping rope had been.

The house was down on Fourth Street. One of those silvered wood, old-as-the-hills structures it'd be awfully hard to call a home, even if you planted geraniums at every window and hung lace curtains.

"I'm scared," I whispered to nobody in particular, though Evelyn Sue, being the only other one in the car, received it.

"It'll be all right," she said, pulling on the emergency brake to make sure we didn't roll down the hill toward Market Street. "Lock your door when you get out. This isn't a good area."

That was a comforting thought. We were in a neighborhood so dark and dangerous that I might get attacked on my way in for an abortion. Great! An illegal abortion. *Swat me to the sidewalk quick and save Evelyn Sue two hundred dollars,* I thought, locking my door before I shut it, looking for muggers. I never did know where Evelyn Sue got two hundred dollars, maybe borrowed ahead against her salary where she was in training as an intern beautician. I'd sure like to have saved her the money if I could have.

We walked up the porch steps together. Stood out there in the middle of Christmas lights rimming the edge of the porch. Evelyn Sue knocked and we waited. It was that time of evening when you know darkness is just around the corner, but instead of looking darker, it just looks misty. Filtered. Like a deep fog is beginning to roll in from the river. Winter twilight.

We stood there until Evelyn Sue's knock was answered. It was a man.

"You said it'd be a woma . . ." I blurted quick, ready to run.

"Is Miranda Fowkes in?" Evelyn Sue asked, firm.

"Just a minute," the man said. When he stepped away from the light even one step, he was gone all the way. Invisible in the dark entry hall.

After several minutes and two cars had passed, a woman appeared in the doorway. She was wearing a housedress that wrapped and tied. Flowered. Dirty over her stomach where she'd smeared her hands.

"You got the money with you?" she asked around a wad in her lower jaw. *Snuff,* I thought.

Evelyn Sue held it out and the woman opened the screen door and took it. We just stood there. "Well, ain't you coming on in?"

We did.

The house held a hickory smell. We could have been right inside a hickory tree itself, the smell was so strong. It made me gag behind my hand because food and strong odors were starting to affect me that way. And I guess the thought of what I was about to do held me tight, too. Going to play God and stop life. I felt like a soldier taking aim at the enemy. Lining up ammunition in this hickory house, setting up an ambush.

We followed her up the stairs, turning to the right at the landing. Two steps more. Into a large room, almost empty, except for a mattress pushed against one wall, a floor lamp, two chairs, and some pictures on the walls. Looked like a room that had once been a bedroom, then had been emptied to make space for a new function.

Why, I didn't know, I suddenly thought of Evelyn Sue in California. The house she'd lived in. It must have been on her mind, too, because she knew immediately when I asked her, "Was it like this?" I looked across to where she stood, tight and tremulous.

"Yes."

"What you say, sugar?" the woman turned to ask.

"Except for the flowered-skirt curtains," Evelyn Sue told me. "They're missing,"

"Look here," the woman's voice shrilled in a rapid ribbon of words, "you making fun of my curtains?"

"Curtains?" I said, squinting up at the windows. "Those are curtains?" Shreds of cloth hanging in the light and yellowed with age. Draped over a curtain rod. The best you could say was they were an attempt at curtains. Not real. Missed the mark altogether.

"Sugar, you just hush and lie down on this bed here," she directed me.

And I moved to do it. Almost lay down, but stopped. It wasn't because of the baby inside me that hadn't moved enough yet for me to feel. Not that. It was a photograph she had on the wall beyond the light that stopped me, because I was moving to lie down when I saw it. A fat little baby with curls down past its ears. Ears poking out through the curls. Those ears were what got to me.

Like an electric current, it shot through me that *that* was what was inside me. Not a bean-size, pulsating, beating, living unhuman something. It was a promise. A promise to look like that. How could I take away its chance to find Earth? I couldn't even throw an unwanted kitten in the Pamlico River, much less deny another human being the right to roam Earth awhile.

Something fierce came into me, cold as a summer radiator and just as uneven and hard. She saw it, too, the woman called Miranda Fowkes did.

"Boudreaux!" she called from where she stood. "You, Boudreaux! Come here!"

But neither Boudreaux nor Sugar Ray Robinson nor the giant that David knocked flat with his slingshot could have stopped me. I backed out the room's door and flung myself down to her two-step landing and all the way, galloping down her long, scarred steps and out the front door before that Boudreaux man ever got off his lazy butt. Heard her shrilling after me. "Sugar! Sugar!"

"Sugar has *left* the house!" I shouted to the cold night. "And she's heading west!"

I was passing the courthouse before Evelyn Sue ever caught up to me. She honked light and I climbed in beside her. "Didya get your money back?" I asked, shivering.

She shook her head.

"Sorry."

"Don't blame you," she whispered.

She turned on the radio and we rode home on the notes of some Nat "King" Cole song about being too young.

17

In September, the fall of 1954, Hurricane Hazel had hit the eastern coast and stirred up trees whose roots went near to the center of the Earth. Just pitched them on their sides, smashing houses in their path.

Well, the third week of December 1955, what hit our house made Hazel look like a mama's girl because the mother of all storms took hold and shook the family tree so hard it like to not withstood it. And we *did* lose an apple or two before it was over and done.

In the first place, Mama hadn't felt well all week. And then there was something changed in my life that made me turn to Daddy instead of Mama. I remembered that, when I sang my solo, Daddy had begun to look at me in a different way. Even with Nicholas coming on the scene Daddy still had some respect for me. And now, especially since he thought I was smart enough to break up with

Nicholas, Daddy looked at me like maybe I was somebody after all. It was a new respect that had come upon him for me, like my becoming a woman slid childhood and its hard-knock life behind me. I felt maybe he'd understand somehow. It was Daddy I needed to tell.

"Daddy," I said on Saturday morning at breakfast.

"Hm-m-m." His voice made its own way around the newsprint and sort of dropped off above the platter of bacon and poached eggs. Definitely didn't want to reach and encourage me to go on.

But doggedly I said it again.

He heaved a sigh and shook the paper so it'd fold nicer and laid it on the corner. I guessed his looking with raised brows meant *go on.*

"Evelyn Sue and I, we've got something we want to tell you." Then I corrected myself. "Need to tell you."

"What in the Sam Hill now? You girls haven't gone off the deep end with some cockamamie scheme to tour Europe on foot, have you?"

I shook my head. This was not going as I had hoped. I pushed the slick white curd of my egg around the plate. Was glad for Evelyn Sue being there. Glad for Grammie visiting Aunt Lacey and Uncle Mac Hall in Virginia Beach these late fall months.

"Well?" He sipped his coffee and set his cup down awkward on the saucer, tipping it plumb over and down the leg of the table. "Good grief! Well, don't just sit there. Go grab me some paper towels!" he barked.

We did. When the mess was cleaned and wiped and all the damage from a spilled half cup of cooled coffee was righted, I began again. Watched the black choreography of shadows from outside where the cords of the wisteria vine growing up the house wall got in the way of sunlight. Where light angled in around them.

"This is hard to tell, Daddy." The paralysis that rises to the throat during trying times came full-fledged, and I couldn't speak or hardly breathe past it.

"Well?" he asked, pouring himself a fresh cup of coffee, which I wasn't even allowed to drink yet, lest it stunt my growth, I reckoned. I wondered, when I told him, if I'd be allowed to drink coffee.

I looked over at Evelyn Sue, who, for about the first time in her life, looked so much like a mother that I was glad all over again she'd come back from the western edge of the continent. A kindness wreathed her face, settling in her wide eyes, and she nodded to encourage me on. After cooking breakfast Mama had gone upstairs to bed with a sick headache. I hated to think what this would do to her. Give it a quarter of an hour and she wouldn't even remember she'd had a headache.

"I'm pregnant." It was easier that way. Instead of saying, *I think,* I just went ahead and threw the truth out there. No thinking to it. Knowing.

Daddy's eyes raised up to meet mine. Then he darted a quick glance at Evelyn Sue, then back to me.

"What's Evelyn Sue got to do with this?" He paused for

an answer and I sucked in my breath to tell him she was supporting me when he asked again. "What?"

I swallowed. It sounded really loud in that quiet room. "She's here to stand by me," I whispered, watching his eyes darting between us.

"Stand by you? Help you? It's a little late for that, isn't it?"

"Yessir."

And then we just sat. The three of us. The house breathed for us because I know we weren't breathing, trying to decide what to do. The pain on my daddy's face was raw. Bold. Then I saw the change coming as he lifted his eyes and fastened me with his new look. The hurt was turning into what I guessed he could live with, anger. His face was turning purple. The anger was building to hurricane force. I could see it but was helpless to stop it.

"Daddy," Evelyn Sue, seeing it too, said in a soothing voice, "Welcome meant I was coming with her to tell you because . . ."

"Coming with her, huh?" He stood and with that eruption his chair fell backwards to the floor. "Why'd she need anybody to come with her? Evidently she's a big enough girl to get herself in the family way, she's big enough to face the music by herself."

I didn't know if he meant for her to leave or not. I wanted her there.

"Stand up!" he shouted at me, though his body didn't

move. Just his voice. He stood ramrod straight. "Stand up!" And I did.

Then he did something he'd never done before, not to any one of his three children. He hauled off and slapped me in the face so hard my spit flew clean over to the sideboard. Little yellow moths flew around me and I sort of staggered a minute.

"Stop!" Evelyn Sue shouted. "Stop that!"

He drew himself up to a full father height and whispered, "And who are you, missy, to be telling me to stop? Aren't you the one who left to go in search of a Hollywood freak? Aren't you the very one? And now look what it's gone and done to your sister . . ." So he knew about Evelyn Sue all along. And somehow connected her bold flight to my dilemma.

"No, sir." I found my voice. "Evelyn Sue didn't have anything to do with this. I did it all on my own . . ."

"Not entirely. I suppose young Canton is the father . . . the bastard."

"No."

He looked at me hard. Drew his head back on his neck. "Then who?"

I shot a look at Evelyn Sue. *Lord knows*, her eyes were saying, *make up somebody if you have to.*

"I don't know." My careful three words found their mark and split him wide open. He pitched back a little, his legs against his fallen chair.

"What's that you say?" he said high and tender, like the next sentence might even be a song.

I realized what that made him think, not naming the father. Like I'd slept with every boy in the county. A tramp. Couldn't help it.

I went to my room and didn't even look over my shoulder. Wanted to say, *I'm sorry, Daddy,* but knew he'd grab it and use it against me. Knew *sorry* was kerosene to the fire, not water. May have looked like water. Clear. But that's where the similarity ended. Looks are deceiving.

18

Mama doggedly decorated a small tabletop tree in the living room. The first time ever we didn't have a ten-foot-tall tree. She hummed along on Christmas carols. "Oh Little Town of Bethlehem" for the lights. "The First Noel," the tinsel. "We Three Kings" as she fluffed on beat-up Lux flakes that she'd whipped to look like snow. Spread it gently on the branches.

But joy was missing from her. She had a struggle just getting all that done. After Daddy told her—he must have told her—she never said a word to me. Not directly to me. As if avoiding it, we'd be halfway to safety. As long as it wasn't given life by her mention, the baby would perhaps evaporate. No words, no breath carrying the truth of a new person coming, and then it won't happen. I'm afraid my mother's logic eluded me. What I needed was for her to just say, "Welcome, no matter what, I love you." Look deep into me with her bright eyes. And then I'd have hugged her tight and said, "Oh, Mama. I'm so sorry. But now, my life is going down this road. Please go down it with me."

Julian and Wysteria came the next day after I'd told Daddy, Julian doing what he always did so well: making sure I felt in my place, which was always going to be beneath him. Far beneath. And, being a person who felt life hinged on what other people said and thought about you, the first thing Julian wanted was for me to have an abortion. Said he knew a woman. I asked him did she live on Fourth Street? Name of Miranda? His eyes quickened and I told him she wouldn't do. That was not for me.

Seeing Wysteria's hard line of a mouth, so quick to condemn, made me suddenly want to laugh. Oh great! Laughing would go over like a lead balloon. I hadn't laughed in a week and a half. Not even smiled. Everybody ought to laugh at least once a day. If you don't, there are streaks inside you that plumb dry up without the oil of laughter.

Right here at Christmas I was remembering that when Mary was pregnant with Jesus, there wasn't a father. Well, it was different, but in one way it was the same. I thought about her and knew the hardness.

"Send her on a trip," Julian finally said to Daddy. That fit right in with Mary's story.

Mama was fiddling with the Christmas tree, adjusting and separating the foil icicles. Silent.

"Send her to Aunt Lacey's in Virginia Beach," Wysteria

chimed in like she was blood kin. "You could swap her off for Grammie after Christmas."

There were no stories this day. Precious little in the way of conversation. Just fragments torn off from people. Fragments thrown out to see if they'd fly. I kept my fragments to myself. Thought of Mary going to Bethlehem. Of the knocking on doors Joseph did.

I thought of the small life growing in my safety. *I am in charge of this life,* the thought suddenly came. *And I mean to stay in charge.*

19

THERE WERE NO PORCH SETTERS THAT LATE IN DECEMBER.
Even in the South. Winter was here for certain. It was two
days past Christmas. I'd put on my coat and struck out for
a long walk. Passed house after house, closed against the
rawness of this wet tail end of December.

One house I passed slowed me down. It was my pediatrician's house. I could see her through the front glass
door. She was sitting beside her little boy as he played the
piano. Through the glass door you could hear the faint
music, but only if you knew what you were listening for.
Mainly high notes.

I sort of lounged on a rock wall across the street and
watched. Listened to the pale notes sliding thin through
the frosty air. Someone passed me but I kept my eyes
on Dr. Irons, with her full head of auburn hair. She was
bent toward the boy playing. Being a mother almost in

pantomime, the music was so muffled.

Someday, I began thinking, *I might be bending over a little boy, encouraging him on, listening to his music,* when the person who had passed me doubled back and stopped between me and the house I was watching.

"Welcome?"

I looked up. It was Randy, a stocking cap hiding his hair. Nose red as Rudolph's.

"Oh . . . hi, Randy."

"I've been meaning to call you since I got home, but . . ." He shrugged.

"I know," I said. "Family."

"Absolutely. And I didn't get in until Christmas Eve. I'm working a job at a filling station up in Raleigh, pumping gas to fill in the gaps. Gives me some running money."

I nodded.

"Whyn't you call me back, Welcome? I called twice this fall." I looked at the ground. "You're not . . . you know . . . in trouble or anything, are you? You'd tell me?"

When I first looked up to his eyes I hung in the same dilemma I'd not really faced yet. It'd sure be easier and wouldn't he *want* to know? Heck, if I'd planted a seed, I'd want to see the results. What grew.

But when I opened my mouth to spill it all, the very bottom of the truth came upon me, and I knew I couldn't do that to him. To me. Forcing yourselves together when you don't match would be a mistake. And tight as the money was for the Newsome family, it'd probably mean

Randy'd have to quit college. That was the card that trumped the board straight across finally. It changed the complexion of the game.

"No, no," I hastily said. "I've just been busier than a one-armed paper hanger . . ."

"With the hives," he finished for me, and we both smiled. Relieved.

"You going my way?" I asked, turning to go home.

"Well, I could I guess, but actually I'm running to the store for my mama. She's fixing those fluffy candied yams and needed some shredded coconut . . ."

I smiled. "We had those, too. They're the best."

He nodded. Then started jogging backwards, still watching me.

"Well, I'll see you, Randy," I called. Knew it wouldn't happen. Not ever again. I was fixing to waltz out of his life for good. It seemed odd that a boy who'd only kissed me twice had given me something as important as a baby.

As I turned to cross the street, I heard louder music and looked up to see Dr. Irons playing by herself now. And if you closed your eyes and listened hard, you could almost pick out the tune. It sounded vaguely familiar. One of those songs you've heard your mama humming as she worked around the house. And I started humming it as I walked. Thought the name of it'd probably come to me if I hummed long enough. And though it never did come, the title, I hummed along steady all the way home. Getting in practice.

20

IF MY DADDY HADN'T HAD HIS HEART ATTACK ON NEW Year's Eve, we'd have been celebrating the coming of a new and strange year at Virginia Beach with Aunt Lacey and Uncle Mac Hall. I was to stay there, at least until summer. They'd be swapping Grammie for me. But getting ready that morning, my daddy just fell out across the bed. By the time the ambulance arrived, he was gray as the shirt he was wearing and they whisked him straight off to the hospital. We followed, Evelyn Sue, Mama, and me, but Evelyn Sue and I didn't stay all night since he got pronounced out of the woods.

"He'll be okay, Welcome," Mama told me the next morning when she came home from the hospital to bathe. "But a trip that long'll be out of the question anytime soon." She gathered up her underthings from several drawers, then turned on her way to the bathroom and, as an afterthought, said, "I don't know what we can do about you. Aunt Lacey's expecting you to stay with them until . . ." She let it sort of fade there. Couldn't bring herself to mention a baby yet.

I thought about it a minute. "I could take the bus," I said.

She stopped in her tracks. "Well, now, there's a thought. Do you think you could?" She nodded in answer to her own question. "And Mother could come here by bus. I'll call Lacey tonight." She walked all the way to the bathroom before she turned back to me and, holding me with her eyes, said, "You know . . . I can't figure out what went wrong and where it did."

"What are you talking about?"

She shook her head and went on into the bathroom, its tiled walls hollowing her words. "I always thought we were just about the most . . ."

"Perfect family?" I finished for her.

I didn't hear her answer.

Early the next Tuesday morning, Evelyn Sue drove me to the Trailways station and saw me off, like Lydia Meyers and all the other girls who'd left schools in a hurry . . . saw me off with my two suitcases of clothes, already mostly too tight.

"Bye, Wel!" she shouted, and jumped up and down like she was sending me off to the Olympics, her frosty breath mushrooming out beyond her.

I waved and turned around to watch all the way to the

corner, where my bus turned onto the main highway and I lost sight of her. Then there was nothing to watch but the January landscape out the window. No place on earth as flat and desolate as eastern North Carolina. For a state with mountains that look sharp as the Swiss Alps and lakes and oceanfront beaches that vacationers come for from all over, it sure has a stretch of never-mind territory that the Lord must have forgot on creation day. Silvered tobacco barns, stone chimneys that had lost their houses too long ago to remember, kudzu threatening to take their stones one by one.

In Windsor we stopped and I went into the bus terminal to go to the bathroom. Forgot my purse was packed in my suitcase in the luggage hole deep in the bus, so I didn't have a coin for the stall. Couldn't decide if I should crawl under the partition. About that time a black lady came in.

"They all full?"

I shrugged. "I don't think so."

"Well, you go ahead and go in first. I'll wait."

"No, ma'am."

So she dropped her money in and did her business. When she came out I tried to grab the door, but she was so quick she let it slam before I could stop her.

"Shucks!" I grunted.

Then she looked at me like she was seeing me for the first time. "Lord have mercy. You didn't bring your purse and you're stuck, aren't you?"

I nodded.

"I've been there myself. Let this be on me," she said, like she was buying me lunch.

She dropped the nickel in the slot and, smooth as oil, I slid into that small stall that held relief for a built-up bladder with a baby resting on it.

When I came out she was gone and I didn't even get to thank her. I climbed onto the bus and sat back in my seat when, lo and behold, on she climbed.

"Well, I'll be smacked!" she said, grinning big like we'd been best friends all our lives. "You beat me out here. Are we going the same place?"

I patted the seat beside me. "Would you like to sit here?" I asked.

She smiled again. Wasn't all the time blacks sat with whites on public transportation, though I had read in the paper in December about a woman named Rosa Parks down to Alabama holding forth. Said she'd sit where she would. Got arrested for it, too.

"You sure?" she asked, a smile quivering the corners of her mouth.

"Oh, please. You saved my life in there. It's the least I can do."

And that's how I came to know Hattie Bernice Mercer. Windsor's near the state line, so, by the time we were deep in Virginia, we'd come to be easy with each other. Covered the weather. Christmas.

"So how come you traveling north?" she asked me.

"To see my aunt and uncle. To stay with them a while." My hand slid, like it was drawn, to my waist. Already reaching out to hold what was sleeping inside. "And you?" I asked her.

"Well, I got a errand I go on every January."

"An errand?"

She nodded and looked down to her hands, folded in her lap. Waited a long time before she said more. I'd begun to look out the window when she said, "It's my son's birthday. January fifth is."

"How old is he?" I asked, but had sensed enough from her voice not to whoop it up big. Just asked.

"He'd be thirty if he'd lived."

I turned and looked at her face.

"What happened?" I whispered it. I didn't remember ever meeting anybody who'd lost a child before. And with my growing situation, that somehow carried more weight now.

She gathered thoughts and memories a while before she told me. Finally she said, shifting her eyes to the back of the seat ahead of us, "It was the summer after his first year at the seminary. He was studying to be a preacher."

Her eyes found mine on that but went right back to the seat in front of us like that seat held the words she was going to say. "He did summer mission work, was helping with a Vacation Bible School in a church up to Norfolk. A big church downtown and they just loved him." Again she had touched eyes with me.

"One day, earlier in the week, he had tore up his bed-sheet and gave each of the children in his group a piece of that sheet. Said, 'Now you go out in this churchyard and put the most beautiful thing you can see inside this cloth and bring it to me. I'll close my eyes,' he told them and counted to one hundred. And you know what they done?"

I shook my head no.

"He called me that night to tell me. Said they snuck around behind his back and when he opened his eyes they all fell on top of him, put their little cloths all around him. Told him he was the most beautiful thing they could find."

I smiled at her. "Sounds like the way I felt about a teacher we had once."

"Then you know what I'm saying. Well, that last morning of Bible School he and his roommate were running late and they knew all them young'uns was waiting for them. So they rushed along on this two-lane road when their wheels sort of went off onto the side of the road, off the pavement."

She stopped. I reckon she was seeing it in her head now. Made me wish I'd never asked the question. But then, maybe she'd needed to tell somebody this day.

"The patrolman, he said they overcorrected. Tried too hard to get back to the pavement. Flung them directly in the path of a large truck."

She shook her head slow.

Our bus ground on through the bleak January morning.

Eating up highway. Throwing us to this side, then that, with its dips and curves. The sound was bigger than any of us. Somewhere along this highway my bus would pass Grammie's bus heading south, and neither of us would even know we'd come that close to each other.

"I'm so sorry," I said and wanted to reach over and pat her hand to comfort her. Finally did and a tear splashed down on my hand. Hers. Her tear. I couldn't see out the window anymore myself. It was blurred.

"There are simply things you remember on a birthday that you don't 'specially think of the rest of the year," she went on at last. "Firsts. The first pat-a-cake, first smile, the way he turned at the end of the street on his first day of school. Stepped apart from his little buddies and turned to wave to me. Then went on."

We didn't speak for a long time, then I said, "There is nothing I can say to help. I know that." Could feel my chin quivering. Kept on anyway. "But I'd like to tell you something. The reason I'm going to Virginia is to have a baby." Then added, "Nobody else knows hardly."

She quick looked up. A smile cracked through and, after she'd memorized my face good, she heaved over and hugged me, patting my back over and over. Nobody. Nobody had done that for me and I needed it, I guess, because I started bawling in earnest . . . and bawled and bawled.

Then, Lord, she told me so many things, tricks to remember, like:

"Now when you go to burp him, set him up and hold him right up under his arms with one hand. Acrost his chest, like so. Lifting the arms brings the burp."

"Yes, ma'am."

"And when he gets wiggly while you're changing his diaper, and they do get wiggly, you just say nursery rhymes to him to hold on to his attention."

"Yes, ma'am."

"You know any nursery rhymes?"

"No'm."

"I'll send you a book of them."

I wished for a pencil to write it all down. Never heard so many tips. She could have written the Bible on child-raising.

"And you going to live in Virginia? From now on? Or you gonna give your baby away? You ain't gonna do that, are you, because Hattie's been giving you her hard-earned tips free and for nothing if you're gonna give him away."

"No, ma'am," I said. "That's decided. Hard. Firm. I'm not giving my baby to anybody else to raise. What you told me I'll remember and use." And I believed that to be true. "Gonna live with my aunt and uncle, I expect, til I can get on my feet."

She just watched me, smiling. Like she knew. Everything.

"Ten minutes to Virginia Beach," the driver said over his microphone.

"Well," I said, wiping my face on my coat sleeve, where

the dried tear streaks felt stiff, "I don't even know your name. Mine's Welcome Marie O'Neal."

She didn't flinch or take exception to my name. Just said, "And mine's Hattie Bernice Mercer."

People all around us were stirring and gathering things. The two of us were an island, sitting there inside our friendship.

"My friends all call me Hattie," she added as an afterthought.

And then something came to me. So amidst all the confusion of entering the city and braking for stoplights and wailing sirens streaking up one side of the city and down the other, I turned to her. "Hattie, what was your son's name?"

"Adam." And it was almost holy the way she whispered it.

I swallowed hard. Not because it would be a promise difficult to keep, but because I wanted her to know where it came from. Deep inside.

"I wonder," I began hesitantly, "would it be okay?" Then halted. It was really going to be what Grammie labeled presumptuous. Shouldn't have started to tell it. And anyway, I could go ahead on my own and do it and she'd be none the wiser.

"What?" she asked. "What you wonder?"

"Well . . . if I happen to have a boy, a son?" She nodded and I noticed how her eyes quickened. She knew before I said it. "If I have a son, I would like to call him Adam."

Her eyes told it all. And though they spilled over, they never lost touch with mine. She finally shook her head and I said, "If that's okay, I mean."

"Oh, it's . . . beautiful. Fine and beautiful and . . . exciting to know there'll be another Adam growing somewhere on this planet. My Adam would just love it."

And before we got off the bus I gave her my aunt and uncle's street address and she wrote down her address for me so I could send her a picture when the baby came.

I promised I would.

Part Two

21

January in Virginia was no better than it was near the coast in North Carolina. Bleak and cold.

Uncle Mac and Aunt Lacey saw to it that I felt right at home, though. They revamped their basement family room for a private bedroom for me, with a half bath to myself. Tried to overcome the negatives in this new situation by laying out a lot of positives.

My Aunt Lacey was not without heart. She was at least a decade younger than Mama. Maybe that was why her eyes still danced with warmth. She had more energy. She was the one who suggested I use her car. So, I did. Borrowed it twice, driving down to the beach, where I sat bundled up against a dune for protection from the wind. The second time I watched the ocean for hours, felt its rhythm deep and urgent, pounding the sand as it rocked. Thought of the living things in that ocean. Small as clams, clear as jellyfish, large as whales. Smelled its saltiness and whispered my secrets to it.

"I'm afraid," I told it. "There's only one door for this baby to come through. And I'm small and a baby's head is big. What happens? Does a person just split to accommodate? Do many people die from that happening?"

No answers came, though I waited. Only sea gulls screeching like unoiled metal, foam staying behind on the sand after the wave went back. A veil of sand clinging to my skin wherever I rested a part of me. And filling my ears was always the roar.

"Is it noisy inside you?" I asked of the ocean. Then blanched at the thought that I must have been considering entering the water and walking until I left life.

No, I wasn't! Thank God I knew that. What I *was* wondering was if it is silent in the ocean of the womb. If the baby floating inside hears a roar or voices of people, like they are in the next room. If my baby's ears were even formed yet. Its fingernails. Its hair.

So I decided to go to the library and check out a book on the development of the fetus in the womb, so every single day I'd know what was happening.

"May I help you?"

"I'd like to get a library card, please."

"May I see your driver's license?"

I showed her.

"It's North Carolina," she said.

"Yes. I'm just here for about six months."

"And with whom do you live?"

I didn't think that was anybody's business. But I did tell her nicely, by saying, "My address is 435 Gotham Road."

"Do you live there alone?"

"Why?"

She blinked. "You're a minor and we need to know whom to contact if you don't return your books."

"I'll return the books. Book. I only want one today."

"That may well be the case but we have to know . . ."

I understood.

"I live with my aunt and uncle, Lacey and Mac Hall."

She dragged out the thick Virginia Beach/Norfolk/Chesapeake phone book and verified it, I guess, because I got a library card and a book. But when I sat back in the car, I could feel my swallowed-down anger. I thumbed through the book, which was mostly about how to take care of a newborn, not what was happening week by week before birth. I was too tired to go back in the library. Seemed I slept or felt like I needed to all the time. And I was still mad because I'd had to give out personal information. Being pregnant made me want to be private. Very private.

When I got to the place where Gotham Road turned off of Virginia Beach Boulevard, I drove into the Parkette Drive-In, which was on the corner.

The carhop, on skates (this was a new thing, didn't have them back in Lily), took my order.

"Fries."

"That all?"

I nodded.

"Nothin' to drink?" She batted her round eyes twice while she waited for my head shake. Worked on a piece of gum. Her nametag said *Gloria.*

"No thanks, Gloria."

She skated off.

I was almost asleep by the end of the five minutes it took to fry those skinny potato parts.

"Here ya go!" her cheerful voice said.

"Thanks." I paid her plus a small tip.

"I brought ketchup just in case," she pointed out. "And water." Two paper cups, one small, sat to one side of the tray. The small one was half filled with ketchup. I thanked her and off she rolled.

In trying to bring the cup of ketchup to a more manageable level so I could dip without raising my arm above my shoulder, I tipped it and spilled myself a lapful of ketchup. All over the front of my one and only skirt that still buttoned and zipped.

That was when I discovered she'd brought no napkins. Oh, great!

I pushed the call button.

"Can I he . . . ou?" a nasal voice squawked, losing parts of words. No wonder that was a backup system.

"Could you send Gloria out?" I left off the *please,* I was so irked.

Then I waited for her to come. *Should have said with nap-*

kins, I thought. While I waited I began eating the french fries, dipping them into the Red Sea in my lap, which was more accessible than I had bargained for.

After a couple of minutes passed (seemed like five but was two on the car clock), I pressed *call* again.

"Can I help you?"

"Is Gloria on her way?"

"Gloria?" Then the voice turned away from the mike and asked someone nearby where Gloria was.

I mean they weren't busy. I was one of two cars there. What did it take!

"Gloria's . . . to the . . . est room. She'll . . . out direct . . ."

Whether it was the Virginia pronunciation of *out*, sounding like *oot*, or just the stupidity of the situation, I don't know to this day. If I'd had a baseball bat, I'd have taken out the squawk box. I remember that much.

"Get your skates on." I started low and slow. "And get out here to this green Pontiac. On the double. And bring with you . . ." By now, even if her end of the squawk box was as defective as mine, she should have been able to hear me without the benefit of the microphone, "a handful of napkins!"

The manager came. A weary-looking man. Too weary to skate, he came on foot. With enough napkins to start up my own concession in their parking lot.

As I ate the rest of my french fries, I tried to sort out why I kept getting so angry so fast. My feelings were certainly near the surface, that was for sure.

I drove the two blocks home thinking maybe I was learning to stand up for myself. And next, the baby. That's what parents do—stand up for their kids. I didn't even look over my shoulder at the shadow that followed me when I got out of the car. The shadow that crept behind me contained enough bad feelings to stay a flat, dark shadow that would grow in size during the next months as the baby grew within me. I completely ignored it and called out to my Aunt Lacey as I crossed the threshold, "Do you think you could check out a library book for me?"

22

THE INVISIBLE HOURS OF THE NIGHT, REAL BUT RARELY seen except by insomniacs, were all mine. Being without friends for one week. Then two weeks. I stopped dreaming because I was sleeping my deep-sleep hours and then waking up. There was none of that fringe time. Those extra hours when I could dream out my madness so it didn't leak into my real life. My waking life. Sometimes I was sure I was going crazy from sadness and loneliness. My aunt and uncle weren't nearly enough. Not for me.

And my senses were going lame at the same time. At least *touch*. I longed, hungered for someone to touch me. An arm around my shoulders. A hard rub saying someone outside my body cared. I drove downtown on a weekend and parked. Got out of the car and walked the sidewalk just to be jostled by the crowd. To feel human friction and know I existed.

Mama called every Saturday morning.

"Just checking on you, Welcome," she said. "Are you doing all right? Do you need anything?"

You, I wanted to say, but of course I didn't.

"How's Daddy?"

"Oh, he's improving. They've found high blood pressure and are trying to treat that, too. They're letting him go back to work part-time next week. You know, you probably need to go ahead and make an appointment to see an obstetrician, Welcome."

It was the closest she'd come to acknowledging my baby.

"I have."

"When?"

"Next Thursday. It's about six blocks from where we are, so I'll walk, since both Aunt Lacey and Uncle Mac will be at work. It's good for me to walk, you know."

Then, business all taken care of, we sat. Me picturing her sitting at the hall telephone table, little round cherry table, holding the black phone, Lily's thin telephone book in the curving drawer.

"I'm sitting at the kitchen counter," I told her so she could place me.

"What's the weather like?"

"Snowed two days ago but didn't stick. Pretty raw and cold."

"When it starts in good weather you might want to get Lacey to take you to a rummage sale. I'll send you a little money for it when it gets warmer."

I didn't ask the questions I needed to be asking. Only thought of those questions years later. Things like, *Are you-all all right? I mean financially with Daddy being off work? Couldn't you get Julian to help you out a little? After all, you sent him to college and then three years of law school.* I didn't know to ask them, though, so we just sat in spaces of quiet and hummed our own thoughts.

"Oh, look who just came down the stairs all sleepy-eyed . . ." she said.

"The creature from the deep," I said and by then Evelyn Sue had stuck the receiver under her sleep-wadded hair and heard me.

"And who is this?" she croaked. "The wild and woolly woman from Virginia Beach?"

"Yeah," I growled.

With my mama you were called upon to be solemn, serious, heavy. Try to be cute and she either took it seriously and missed the point and wept or didn't understand and the conversation got too confusing for words and you learned not to use those words again. With sisters you can growl.

"How's babee?" she asked.

"Quiet."

"Won't be long and you ought to feel movement, huh?"

"I guess. I'll ask the doctor when I go Thursday."

"Aha!" She coughed to one side then came back to say, "I hope he has big fingers . . . the doctor."

"Oh, thanks."

I could hear Mama, still sitting on the telephone chair, say, "Ask her how Lacey and Mac are."

"How are Aunt Lacey and Uncle Mac? Mama wants to know. Actually, I don't give a happy hoo-hoo *how* they are . . ."

Mama again. "Evelyn Sue, you ought to be ashamed . . ."

"I'm putting Mama back on," Evelyn Sue said. "It's great talking to you but I gotta get a cup of coffee before I pass out here in the front hall. Love ya!"

"Loves ya," I said back the way I used to when I was little and I'd follow her around screaming, "Ella Sue!"

"Well, I'm back," Mama said. "What's Lacey up . . ."

"Mama." I don't know what made me say what I did. Nothing conscious and everything subconscious. "I want you to know something. Because my not saying who the father of my baby is made it sound like I don't know. That's not true. I do know, but unless I decide to ever tell *him*, I'm sure not telling anybody else. But it's not the whole county. I'm not a loose girl. I could tick off names for you on the fingers of both hands, naming girls in my class who are loose. I'm not one of them. This was a one-time thing."

I stopped right there. Telling this to a woman who was a virgin right up to her wedding night probably didn't help her one tiny bit. One or one hundred times—all the same to her.

But you know what she said? She gathered a deep

breath. I heard it come and go and then she said, "I understand, Welcome."

It was kind, whether she really did or not . . . understand.

And I said, "Well, I'd better jump off of here and go help Aunt Lacey with making the beds and doing the laundry. Tell Daddy hi for me and call me again."

"Oh, I will."

And she did.

Every Saturday morning.

23

THE DOCTOR HAD BIG HANDS. BUT THAT WASN'T important after all because, even though it hurt some when he did the pelvic exam, he was the kindest man. Told me what to expect. What to feel for. Said we were doing just fine.

"You're twelve weeks," he said. "Let's say-y-y . . . we'll be looking for them on July sixteenth or thereabouts."

"Them?"

"Triplets. Didn't I say?"

"Triplets. Sweet Jesus!"

He roared with a deep, growling laugh and I knew I'd been had. But I played along. "All boys?"

"Absolutely," he said, pleased I'd jumped right in with him. "The triplets are boys. The other two are girls."

I nodded. "Good. Five in all. Some of each."

"I'll see you in one month," he said.

I put my clothes back on and asked the receptionist to mail me the bill. Lord knew how I'd be paying it with no job in sight. Then I made the next appointment for a month later and walked home, where two wonderful things awaited me. The first one, already there. The second to come.

When I looked through the fistful of mail I set on the dining room table, there was a letter addressed to me with a Raleigh date stamp. And the return address said *H. Mercer.* Ah! She did write me like she said she would.

> *Dear Welcome,*
>
> *By now I suppose you are all settled in. I hope so. Are you getting rounder and rounder with the little one? In a separate box I'm sending you a nursery rhyme book I promised you. It's the very one I read to my Adam and next summer you'll be reading it to your Adam. (Or Eve?) It pleases me to do this and it's yours to keep. Forever. Also, in the box are clothes. Several large shirts. I went to a rummage sale, where I picked up some clothes for you and the baby. When you bust out of your own wardrobe, you'll have a starter wardrobe.*
>
> *Well, I'd better be finishing here and go eat my supper. I've had a pot of navy beans simmering all evening and I expect they're about ready. Got*

cornbread cooking in my spider pan in the oven.
Wish you could come join me. I'd set an extra
place in a heartbeat.

Hattie

Maybe I would one day. Maybe I'd ride a bus to Raleigh
and take Adam to go see her. Maybe I just would. I could
close my eyes and smell those beans on her stove right
then.

I folded up the letter and pushed it back into its envelope. Didn't want to lose her address. Wanted to show
Aunt Lacey when she got in from work.

I set the table and unloaded the dishwasher. Moved all
the mail to the kitchen bar first. As I did, I became aware of
noises from out back coming through the closed windows
of the house. Shrieks of laughter. Words being yelled. When
I went to the kitchen window, I saw a wild game of basketball going on in the back yard that butted up to ours.

A boy, a girl, and a woman were fighting for control of
the ball. Every time it went up, the boy managed to yank
it from the space above their heads. He shot at the basketball hoop over and over, missing some, making most. But
he was the only one shooting.

The woman and the girl whispered at the side and the
next time the ball sailed aloft, the woman grabbed the boy
and tickled him for all she was worth while the girl shot
the ball.

"No fair! No fair!" the boy yelled. "Mom, that's no fair."

They laughed so hard, the mom and the girl, that they sat right down on the driveway in front of the basketball hoop.

Made me homesick to the point I almost cried, watching a family be just that. A family. I stood and watched and wondered if I'd ever be part of my own family again. I even pulled a kitchen barstool to the window and watched until four-thirty, when Aunt Lacey came home.

"Whoo-whoo!" she hollered as she came through the front door.

"Rejoice!" I hollered back, trying to shake off my blue mood so Aunt Lacey wouldn't know how miserable I was feeling. I don't know what made me choose that word but it seemed appropriate.

"Rejoice?" she asked, coming in the kitchen all smiles. "Rejoice?"

I smiled back. "Two things . . . well, three if you count what's coming. One, the doctor said I'm fine and so are the babies."

"Babies!" She sank onto the nearest stool.

We went through all that about the five, three boys and two girls on the way and whittled it down to one healthy baby.

"Okay. We can live with one," she said, laughing. "And we'll be ready by the middle of July. Now what are numbers two and three?"

"Well, two . . ." I reached over and pulled the envelope

from the stack of mail. "I got a letter from my friend."

"Oh . . ." She opened it and read every word. "How nice. How very nice."

I liked the way Aunt Lacey looked you right in the eye when she talked to you. Not like her older sister, my mama, who was always so busy she often looked only with her ears. Maybe it had something to do with having three children as opposed to having none.

"Sometime let's us have navy beans and cornbread," she said. "It's a good winter supper. What d'ya think?"

"Yeah. And I can cook it. I've watched Mama. I know how."

"Then it's settled. How about Saturday night?"

"And slaw with it?" I asked.

She nodded.

"Aunt Lacey, I don't know how to earn my board here," I said on the spur of the moment. At home it wouldn't have entered my mind to say that. But here it did. "I've applied several places for work but no luck yet."

The Parkette Drive-In was now out since I'd had a small temper tantrum in their parking lot. A person whose life focused on napkins as an essential was probably not going to work out, asking questions like, "Do you want cream with your coffee?" or "Is that a large fry, sir?" I might suddenly go insane and start roller-skating backwards, throwing ketchup in all directions. Nope. The Parkette was out. Anyway, roller-skating while I was pregnant could have been more interesting than I'd care to deal with.

"Now don't you even be thinking about that," Lacey assured me. "We're working that out. You're doing the housework, the laundry, the cooking. You can't begin to know how marvelous it is to come home to a sparkling clean house. I just didn't have time to keep it this clean. That makes your staying here a double pleasure. First, we have you and the joy of having this baby begin its life here with us. Then, we have your contributions as a member of this family. Don't you even think about paying us back. For anything."

Wait'll the doctor bill comes. She might sing a different song then.

"You know, Welcome," Lacey said, sitting across the table from me, "Mac and I always wanted children. It just wasn't in the cards for us. This is wonderful. Our being able to go through it with you. It is our privilege. And your helping around the house is pure gravy."

I *was* being useful. I knew that for a fact. Aunt Lacey was such a people person that she neglected things, which is not a bad way to be. But, since I had no people for the moment, things were it for me. So I dusted all her bric-a-brac, wiped out cobwebs, even Windexed picture frames. Their house was clean as a whistle. That kitchen floor you always hear people talk about eating off of? It was right there on Gotham Road. Due to my hard work. I was getting a full dose of homemaking, my term. (Nicholas's had been *housekeeping*.) It wasn't all bad and it kept me busy. But I was beginning to understand my life might need more than this.

"And what is number three?" Aunt Lacey asked me.

"The box from Hattie Mercer on the way with the book and the new wardrobe."

She smiled. "Well . . . don't stop at three. There's a number four surprise for you."

"For me?"

"After dinner, though. After dinner," she said.

Dinner was a smoked picnic ham I'd stuck into the oven to cook on low heat before I'd walked to the doctor. And yams. And green beans. And a fresh fruit salad I'd cut up right after lunch.

"Tell me, Welcome," Uncle Mac asked as we ate, "so we're all together on this, what is the story we need to stick to? When people ask, and they will, where the baby's father is, the three of us ought to sing the same song, don't you think?"

Coming from my daddy those words might have been sarcastic, depending on his mood. Laced with hidden messages like, "Now that you've thrown us all into this mess, you'd better come up with something good to save face. What we need right here is a save-face story, so what is it?"

But Uncle Mac, saying it in his gentle way, a smile playing around his mouth, well, it didn't put a person off and scare the wits out of them so they couldn't think clear to answer. And his eyes sparkled with a little wicked fun when he said it. Like we were all in this together and it wasn't all that bad.

"Reckon we could say the baby's father is in college elsewhere and I came to live with you-all to have the baby here. How'd that be?" I asked.

Aunt Lacey smiled and said, "I can't think of a better way to put it myself." And her eyes searching mine said she meant it. Every word.

"Well, now that's settled," Uncle Mac said, cutting away at his fourth slice of ham, "and by the way, this is delicious. How're we going to keep her here, Lace, so we can eat like this every night? You have no idea what pitiful meals we come up with when it's just the two of us."

"We eat out a lot," she chimed in.

"Out of necessity," he added.

I noticed Aunt Lacey's eyebrow, her right one, shoot up in an irritated arch. "That's enough, Mac," she said.

But her saying that didn't make a dint in what he was feeling, and he kept right on. That was the way Mac was, I learned, stubborn. Not unkind but surely a person who knew what he felt and said it. Almost always.

"When the best thing on the table is the ice water, you learn rather rapidly the names and locations of good eating places."

The electricity raced right across the table. I could almost see it. When Mama and Daddy argued she always ended up crying. Not so with her baby sister, I found out. She gave as good as she got. And I didn't feel it necessary to leave, either. I sat right there like a spectator at a fight. But not taking sides. Just watching the fireworks.

Aunt Lacey didn't hesitate to enumerate all the things she *could* do, even if cooking wasn't one of them. And Uncle Mac finally agreed that, although he would have loved to have married a woman handy in the kitchen, he was proud she taught in a college and wouldn't honestly change her for the world.

"Honestly?" she asked.

And this was still electricity, but now it was smooth and fast, not bumpy and popping like before.

"What do you think," he said and we all knew it wasn't even a question.

"And," he added, "if we can just figure out a way to keep Welcome and keep her cookin'. . ."

"Oh, I don't think you stand a chance of losing me anytime soon," I said.

"Well, you must be a little homesick?" Aunt Lacey looked at me, frowning. "There are some neighbors I hope you'll meet. They live on the street behind us and our back yards meet. A very interesting family. I think you'll like them. As soon as the weather warms up a bit, maybe you'll see them in their yard. The Horns."

I figured that might have been the family I'd seen playing basketball.

They never said one more word about my baby's origins. Mac and Lacey. You've got to know right here how very much I appreciated their not asking about who that absent father really was. They weren't perfect. Uncle Mac burped around the house, rattling out belches, and growled when he was hungry, and Aunt Lacey needed time to herself and didn't hesitate to tell me or anybody else who pushed her too close when she was in that mood. And it would have been human nature for them to ask about the father of my child. Maybe they were working up to it. Or maybe they understood and respected I'd be having good reasons of my own not to be stating those facts. It felt good to think they respected me. Especially in my circumstances, when it was hard enough to respect myself.

"I am homesick, Aunt Lacey. Don't get me wrong. I appreciate what you're doing for me. So much. I do miss my family and friends, though. But there was no way I could have stayed on in Lily. Mama and Daddy may be having a hard enough time holding their heads up as it is. With me there it would have clean broken them in half. You know?"

Nobody spoke for the moment and I just let my point rest right there on the table. Being pregnant and unmarried was the elephant of problems.

"You know, it's a shame," Uncle Mac said, gesturing with a slice of buttered bread, "that folks have to be so hard on each other. Every person on this earth has made some misstep or two or three . . . hundred. All this is . . . what we're talking about here . . . it's a little innocent baby on the way because of a misstep. The baby ain't the misstep. It don't know holler from hay about how it came to be. When it gets here, you'll see, all it knows is to squawk when it's hungry or wet or messy or cold or hot. That baby ain't never gonna apologize to you, Welcome, for showing up. Now is it?"

I shook my head no then said, "Just think. We'll be sitting here, come July, at the supper table and there'll be a little one right here in my arms. Me eating around it . . ."

"Uh-uh," Aunt Lacey interrupted. "My lap. Me eating around it . . ."

"Oh, no," Uncle Mac hopped in to avow. "You two ladies are wrong, wrong, wrong. *Me* eating around it. Us guys have gotta stick together. Unless, of course, it's a girl. Then, she'll still be in *my* lap."

I smiled at him. "I wonder what it's doing right this minute," I said. "What part of its body is growing. What . . ."

"Oh!" Lacey jumped up like she'd been pinched. "That's the wonderful-thing-to-rejoice-about number four. I brought you the book."

"The book?"

"Yes," she said, scooting her chair back and making a beeline for the living room to retrieve it. "The book about fingernails and hair and all." She walked sideways to explain. "And when they all grow. Your library book didn't address that. Well . . . I went down to the college bookstore and found one that did."

148

"Oh! *That* book," I said. "You found one?"

"Yes. The what's-happening-now book," she said, but out of sight where she was fishing it from her briefcase.

Lacey and Uncle Mac did the dishes so I could sit in the living room and look through the book Lacey bought me.

"A month, thirty days, into a total of two hundred and sixty-six days, which it takes the baby to be ready to be born," I said out loud to myself, then I divided it out on a scrap of paper. "Eight months and twenty-six days. So not quite nine months. Huh."

I read all about the fetus being protected by a sac filled with fluid from the tenth day on. Along about a week or so before Thanksgiving my little baby had crawled into its own sleeping bag of amniotic fluid.

"Finding out good stuff?" Lacey asked as she passed me to shake the tablecloth out at the front stoop.

"Yeah," I told her. "At four weeks the fetus is one quarter inch long."

She stopped and shook her head. "A quarter of an inch . . . think of that!"

"In April it'll be ten inches long . . . so what d'ya guess now . . . maybe five inches?"

"Probably," she said, going through the door to shake the cloth.

I read about the heart starting up some time before the fourth week. And eyes, nose, ears, and arms and legs starting then, too.

"Well, it doesn't say exactly when for fingernails and hair," I complained to myself, but Lacey picked up on it coming back in the door.

"I'll bet there're plenty of books out there about this sort of thing. We'll look for more."

I smiled as she passed on through to finish up with Uncle Mac in the kitchen. But my thoughts were pulling inside my body, watching the small, pulsating child, deep in its sleeping bag, growing by the minute. Gathering up poundage and gray matter for a July arrival.

24

THE BOX FROM HATTIE ARRIVED THE FOLLOWING
Monday. I was home alone and I didn't wait to open it.
Just dove right in and found the book on the very top.

It was an old Mother Goose book with a black-and-
white checked cover. I sat right down on the sofa and read
some of the rhymes out loud.

"'Higgledy, piggledy, my black hen, she lays eggs for
gentlemen . . .'" I read.

I closed the book, then reopened it to the front, and there
inside the front cover was an inscription. It said, *January 5,
1928 . . . For Adam on your second birthday. You are a fine, big
boy and Mommy loves you.*

I stopped right there and put my name and address in
the upper corner of the first page so if it got lost, we'd get it
back. Didn't want to chance misplacing this special book.

Next, I pulled out the clothes. Quite a few shirts. Lots of

baby clothes. A couple of pairs of slacks with elastic panels across the fronts to expand with my belly as it grew. I slid the black pair on then and there. Wore them the rest of the day.

After lunch, I went to the clothesline in the back yard to hang out the wash. Had laundered all the baby clothes in Dreft laundry detergent. It brought a smile to see them hanging on the line, soaking up this suddenly warm winter day's sun.

"Who has a baby?" The question, the girl's voice, startled me, and I looked around to see who had spoken.

"Hi," I replied when I found a girl of maybe thirteen or fourteen standing at the back yard fence directly in back of our house. The girl I'd seen playing basketball. "Me! I'm the one having the baby."

"You don't look it," she replied.

"I know. It's my first and I'm carrying it in my back. At least that's what some woman in the doctor's waiting room told me. As opposed to hers, which jutted straight out front."

The girl smiled. Like she really cared how I was carrying this baby! I wondered why I had even gone into the explanation.

"You home from school?" I asked her, finishing up hanging the clothes.

"Yep. Got a sore throat."

"Stay away from me," I said, only half kidding. "My name's Welcome O'Neal. What's yours?"

"Cindy . . . well, Cynthia Horn. Cindy for short."

I smiled. Clipped the last little nightgown to the clothes-line. Walked over to her. "What grade are you in?"

"Eighth. And you?"

So, it showed I was still sixteen. Being pregnant made no difference in how old I looked.

"I'm a junior in high school. Well . . . when I go back."

"Where's the baby's daddy?" she asked next.

And, since we'd practiced that song and dance, I told her what we'd agreed upon. Lacey and Mac and I. It seemed to satisfy her.

And then a lull sort of presented itself, that turning point that occurs in new conversations where you can say, "It's been nice talking with you," and end it all. I chose not to take that road because she looked a little lonely and, heaven knows, I needed a friend. Besides, Lacey had said they were an interesting family. The Horns. Anyhow, I would have struck up a conversation with a stray cat if I'd seen one.

"Have you lived your whole life in Virginia Beach?" I asked, leaning on the metal fence to take the weight off my swollen ankles. This time of day they had started to be puffy.

"Oh, no. My twin brother, Cliff, and I were born in the Philippines."

"The Philippines! Long way from Virginia Beach."

She nodded. "Yeah! We moved here about five years ago. Our mom is dean of women at a college here."

We sat on our opposite sides of the fence and she picked

blades of grass and split them to make a whistle until one finally worked. As she tore small slits in the grass she unraveled a story that made my life sound as uneventful as a monk's. It turned out her mother and daddy had been captured early during World War II and placed in a prisoner-of-war camp in the Philippines. She and her brother were born there.

"I don't remember a lot about it," she said. "Cliff says he does, but I don't. Funny how two people can go through the same experience and one person remembers in detail and the other person can't remember much at all. Anyhow, I think he's lying."

"Lying? That's a pretty big accusation."

"Yeah. He lies a lot." And she was solemn as stone. "About all I recall is how we ate eggs."

I frowned. People eat eggs with a fork. Did they do that differently in the Philippines?

"My mother would steal them for us," she went on. "She'd go to the jungle part of the camp and find the nests of wild birds. Bring the eggs to us and we ate them raw."

"Raw?" Made my stomach turn just thinking of the slick contents of eggs rolling down a person's throat. "Whole? Raw?"

"Oh, no." She laughed. "I couldn't eat them like that. We'd stick a pin in them. Make two small holes and suck out the insides from the bottom hole."

I sat by the fence and thought about breakfast à la

prisoner-of-war camp. Breakfast, lunch, and dinner, if you could believe Cindy Horn. Maybe she lied, too.

"Could you still eat them that way?" I asked.

"Oh, sure."

Long after we'd parted I thought about what people are called upon to do in their lifetimes. Maybe being unmarried and pregnant wasn't the worst possible thing to happen to a girl, after all.

She did tell me one other thing before we parted. "We made it," she said. "We lived. My mom and brother and me. But not my dad. He'd been injured too badly. He died there."

I wanted to meet her mother and find out where she found the kind of strength that experience must have taken. Courage. I lay across my bed and thought of their plight and, for the first time since I'd come to Virginia, I felt this might turn out all right after all. People can overcome incredible road blocks.

Sleep must have come creeping in because suddenly I heard Lacey's voice. "You got a letter," she said, coming down the four steps from the living room to hand me an envelope.

I followed her back up the stairs and sat on the sofa to read it. "Well, I'll be," I said. "It's from Daddy."

Lacey was darning socks and I saw her pause just a beat, then start back up again. I read it over to myself one more time.

Dear Welcome,

You've been gone from home five weeks now. Sometimes when I pass the open door to your room, I stop and look in. There are all your stuffed animals and newspaper clippings thumbtacked to your bulletin board. Just seems you might fly right on in like old times.

I hope you are doing well. Your mother tells me she talks to you every Saturday morning.

Maybe we'll get up there to see you one day soon.

Love, Daddy

It was a gift. That letter. I sat there and tried my best to think what I'd ever given him and couldn't for the life of me remember a single thing. At Christmas Mama had always bought the gifts for Daddy. Finally. Yes! A salt-and-pepper shaker for Father's Day. I'd been seven or eight. The salt shaker was a man's head and the pepper was his bow tie. He never used it, though. Put it on a whatnot shelf in the living room. So I guessed I'd never really given my daddy anything.

Yet.

But now I could. My gift might be to show him I'd be the mother to end all mothers. He'd be proud of me when I got done with that kind of gift. If I could do it.

25

THE REST OF THE MONTH OF FEBRUARY SPUN BY. SNOW fell. Not that it stayed. Two consecutive days it fell. But it did remind me what season we were stuck in. Another good report from my doctor. And still Mama called every Saturday morning to check on me.

"Ran into, you'll never guess who, when he was home over last weekend," she said in her usual unraveled way.

I waited.

"Well, don't you want to guess?"

"Hm-m-m," I stalled, thinking. Probably Nicholas Canton but I didn't want to say it. "Saint Valentine," I finally guessed.

She laughed then said, "Randy Newsome. He said be sure and tell you hello when I told him . . . well I said you were in school up in Virginia."

"College of hard knocks," I said, knowing if I ever made it to real college, it'd be after a year and a half more of high school.

It wasn't until March, the middle of the month, that I began to really feel like a piece of a jigsaw puzzle put inside the wrong box. We had done that all the time at our house. Somebody'd pick up a piece off the floor. "Looks like Stratford-upon-Avon," they'd say and lift the lid and toss it in. When in reality it was a part of a scene with sailboats and a boy in New England. Never would fit in Stratford-upon-Avon.

I was that spare piece.

Lacey got moody and kept to herself. Every evening we ate together as always, the three of us. But then she went to her bedroom and shut the door. I supposed she had all she could take of people at school and was ready for solitude when she hit the front door. Even Uncle Mac didn't know what to do with her. I guessed the newness of my being there had just about worn off, which meant I spent evenings down in my room. The weather was cold again and I didn't see any of the Horns. I hated to knock at their door after only one afternoon's conversation with one member of the family. That doesn't quite qualify you as a friend. I'd stand at my patio door and look out at the winter sky holding its stars tight against its blackness.

During those bleak days I read mostly. But regretted, too. Wished for that afternoon in Pullen Park back. Wanted to pull it backwards through the knothole of time and shake it out and do that October afternoon over again.

I called Evelyn Sue often and just talked to her. That made it easier. I always reversed the charges so I wouldn't be even more beholden to Lacey and Mac.

For the most part, the baby hung silent in my ocean and I sometimes wished it gone. Just a disappearance. Not a death. "Oops. It's not a baby after all. A tumor the size of a cantaloupe. Monday we'll remove it. At six A.M. How's that?"

That would be wonderful. That's what.

But time doesn't invert and winter brings on moods and babies cling to their snug rooms altogether too long.

One Friday afternoon the girl named Cindy finally did come over. And after several more times of her coming, I visited her. I wondered how her mother would take to a pregnant girl being friends with her daughter. I know *my* mother would have dusted off her "not our kind of people" speech. And, oddly enough, *I* was supposed to be her kind of people. My mama's. Not that she was particularly proud of it. Of me.

But Cindy's mom was fine with my coming. Warm and friendly and interested in other people. Cliff, Cindy's twin brother, was tall for fourteen. And a little shy but nice enough.

"Mrs. Horn!" he called to his mother.

She poked her head through the open kitchen door. "Yes," she said, sliding her voice around to be sarcastic at being paged like that. "You could say *Mom* or *Mother*, you know."

"Oh, Mater . . ."

She closed her eyes to let the teasing bounce off her.

"Could we have some hot chocolate?"

"Hm-m-m-m," Cindy added in agreement. "With marshmallows."

"All right with me," Mrs. Horn said and went back to whatever she was doing. Which meant *fix it yourself*. At our house Mama would rather fix it for you so you didn't make a big mess. Not so at the Horns'. I guessed when the mother had a job outside the home, you just had to do more around the house. I'd noticed that Cindy vacuumed and Cliff washed the car on warm weekends. Sort of teamwork over at the Horns'.

We were hot in the middle of a long game of canasta but put it on hold while we made our hot chocolate.

Back at the card table, I picked up my cards.

"Someone messed with my hand," I announced immediately. Not only were two key cards missing, the remaining cards were out of order.

"It was Cliff," Cindy said without hesitation.

"Nope." He bounced the word right back at her but didn't look up from studying his hand.

"Well . . . I'm not playing until we get this straight." It made me mad as fire.

That was when Cliff glanced my way. His eyes weren't steady though. They met mine, but looked over at Cindy

160

immediately, then back at his hand. His eyebrows raised.

"See," she hissed. "I'm not kidding, Welcome. Cliff did it. Look at him. Can't you tell?"

His closed mouth sucked in under his front teeth and he began rocking ever so slightly from his waist up. Front to back. Front to back.

I laid my cards down. Face up. "I fold," I said, using a poker term. But I knew he'd get the picture.

He looked up. The rocking stopped. In a quick, bolt-of-lightning move he stood, bringing the table up with him and dumping it all in our laps and on the floor. Then, without so much as an *I'm sorry*, he turned and stalked out of the room.

"Mom!" Cindy shouted and left to find her mother.

Fifteen minutes later, Cindy and I were at our house to finish the canasta game while Mrs. Horn gave Cliff the third degree. That's what Cindy called it.

"He's always doing stuff like that," she said.

"Cheating?"

"Yes. And copying homework. Mom says it's a hard time for a boy. Being fourteen and not having a dad. But I say he's pushing it. He's going to the limit because Mom is trying to understand. He's taking advantage."

"What if she punished him?" I asked.

"Oh, she does. She will. He'll be grounded with no TV for a week for what he did."

Oh, great. I was feeling lousy for being part of that when the phone rang. I ran to the kitchen to catch it. It was Aunt

Lacey from work. Her voice sounded different, strained.

"We just got a phone call from your brother, Julian," she told me. "Your daddy collapsed at home shortly after one o'clock. They rushed him to the hospital and he's in critical condition. Had a stroke, best the doctors can determine. They're going to run tests once they get him stabilized." She paused, I reckon to draw a breath because she'd said it all so fast. "I'm sorry to have to tell you this, Welcome."

"Yes, ma'am."

Maybe some people absorb information at the same time they are seeing how it affects them. Not me. First I have to hear to understand what happened. Then I'll slowly figure out how I stand to change. What I'll be called upon to do.

"I think you ought to go, Welcome. To Lily to see your daddy. I believe there's time."

Time? "Okay."

"Mac and I can drive home to get you and the three of us will head south. We should reach Lily about suppertime."

"Yes, ma'am."

"You might want to pack your Sunday outfit for church." Why did she say that? "We'll be home shortly."

I hung up the phone and stood by myself in the kitchen before I went back to the living room and the canasta game that would stop for good now. I thought about my daddy down in Beaufort County Hospital. Heard Aunt Lacey's wind chimes out on the cold back stoop, making winter music to discard because nobody knew to listen for it.

I almost drowned in the sudden missing. I'd never wanted my family so bad in my life. Wanted the smells of bacon cooking of a morning and the sound of wind coming straight from the coast, making that old house on Main Street creak like an old but seaworthy ship. I missed Lily and everybody in it. Homesickness is well named because it can make a person's body sick. I wanted my daddy.

And then I felt it. No. Yes. There again. No. Again! A small fist inside me feeling the dimensions of its room and giving warning of new life to come.

26

We went straight to the hospital. Second floor. In the annex. The room wasn't hospital white. It had dark wood paneling on all four walls. When we got there Mama was sitting in a straight chair and Julian was in the recliner.

I was shocked to see my daddy. He'd lost so much weight since January. His head, turned to one side, looked like an apostrophe lying loose from a sentence on the white pillow.

Mama hugged me, and my brother, Julian, shook hands with Uncle Mac and hugged Aunt Lacey. While they all hugged and cried a bit together, I walked over to the bedside and stood looking down at my sleeping daddy. He had a bottle of saline solution hanging from a pole, dripping life into him. But not much because he held deathly still. Except for breathing.

Mama came over and said to him, "Walter, Welcome's here. Walter?"

I took hold of the arm without the needle in it and squeezed his hand a little. He opened his eyes and tried to focus on Mama. Then he turned his head my way.

I will say, when he took me in and could really see who I was, a light came on behind his dark eyes. And while Uncle Mac and Mama and Lacey and Evelyn Sue talked in low whispers and Julian cranked out some business phone calls on the telephone in the room, like this wasn't a sick-room after all, my daddy started up telling me things he'd been telling everybody his whole life through. I knew it'd be those stories, but this time I hungered for them. To hear it all, every bit. From day one. He started slow and picked up speed, talking faster and faster to work it all in. He told me about when he was a little boy and how he trapped tadpoles and lightning bugs. And about meeting Mama when he was thirteen and how she'd been the prettiest girl in the whole school.

I listened hard, too, he was so earnest about it. When he got to the part about his last baby daughter being born I thought I'd split apart, it was so beautiful. He told how I'd had one eye closed, winking at everybody, when the nurse brought me out to show me off.

And I held my daddy's hand that night and listened and paid no attention to Julian when he turned to Uncle Mac and said, "That started about four-thirty. He's lost the ability to produce words. It just went. It may come back

but the doctor said probably not. He just makes sounds,"
Julian said. "No real words. It's like a foreign language."

But I heard the words, maybe from remembering all
those stories, and my daddy knew I heard him. He talked
until he fell back asleep. It was all right that I didn't get
to say the things I wanted to tell him—about the baby
moving and when it came I'd be the best mama ever. It
was all right. He'd said what he needed to say.

And later, back at Mama's, when the telephone rang a
little after two in the morning, I turned in my bed, my
very own bed in my old room, and I half sat up to hear
what I already knew.

Julian answered it. "Yes," I heard him say from the bottom of the stairs. Then a long period of silence. "Oh . . .
okay. We'll come right away. . . . I'm sorry, Mama."

And as I lifted up to listen, that small new person
knocked deep inside me again to say that all was well,
and that life is a circle and even before one life ends another one has begun.

27

Aт THE FUNERAL I DIDN'T TAKE OFF MY LONG, FULL
coat. So nobody even guessed. I sat between Grammie and
Evelyn Sue. And I heard nothing of what went on. Only
what was inside my own head. My daddy's last words to
me. He'd told me his father was strict. I know that's what
he said. And that's why he was so hard on me and caused
the separating to begin between us.

The way he told it to me let me know he knew I loved
him even through our differences. He knew. I was hoping
he didn't blame me for his death. Trying to feel sure I
didn't upset him so bad with my news that he started a
decline that ended here.

And Uncle Mac and Lacey drove us home to Virginia
Beach that afternoon . . . after I'd held Mama tight and
whispered she'd be all right. I didn't know, though, if
she would.

"You're surrounded by strong people," Lacey told her, and we left.

On the drive back I told myself that we probably can survive anything. Look at Cindy and her family. Somehow you keep on. Who knows where you get the strength. It's just there when you actually need it.

I sort of knew that, too. About myself.

28

LATE IN MARCH, ON A SUNNY SATURDAY, LACEY ROSE out of the mood she'd been in and the two of us went in search of a rummage sale. Came back with the car loaded.

"Mac! Uncle Mac," I called as I came through the doorway.

"Yoo-hoo." He padded down from the upstairs in his sockfeet.

"Aunt Lacey wants help unloading the car."

He slid on a pair of shoes he kept by the kitchen door. Grinning beneath his mustache, he said, "What'd you girls do . . . buy out the town?"

I carried light stuff. Baby clothes. Blankets. Lacey brought a plastic tub to bathe the baby in and pushed a carriage with her other hand.

Uncle Mac got the collapsed baby crib.

"Got it for seventeen dollars," I told him.

"Weighs too much for seventeen dollars," he said. "Where you want it?"

"Down in my room."

Then he went back for the chest of drawers.

The following week I washed the new baby clothes in Dreft laundry detergent. Painted the baby crib out on the patio. And the chest. Lined the drawers in the chest with scraps of wrapping paper Lacey had saved from forty-two years of birthdays, she said. What a week!

I told Lacey Mama was going to send me some money and I'd give it all to her to pay her back for the rummage sale things.

"That's all right, Welcome," she told me, but I told her back how bad I felt at not having any money to give her that day.

"We needed a crib, Welcome. And a chest of drawers."

And we did. But I hate to owe people and that thought just lay in a corner of my mind.

Missing my daddy was part of every day. Just because he was dead, just because we'd had our differences, didn't mean he'd left my thoughts. His death was heavy, a weighty thought that sank me before my feet hit the floor every morning. *Oh . . . that's it,* I'd think, trying to name the sadness holding me back. *That's what it is.*

Cindy, having lost her father, sort of understood. Especially with the trouble Cliff was having. He'd hardly said two words to me since that day he'd cheated at cards.

Though Cindy never really knew her dad, she named things she missed even now, one April Saturday while we played canasta. Cliff and his mom were at a baseball game and it was just the two of us. Had her whole house to ourselves.

"I miss my dad physically, of course," she said. "Things I never got from him. At least that I remember. His hugs. His laugh. His voice. I think it wouldn't have been deep. Just middle of the road. I'll miss him not being around when I get ready to go on my first date, to my first dance."

We sat in silence. Cindy looking to all that would lie ahead of her without a dad. Me watching out the rear window of my mind to all those things I'd left behind. Same things, just different places in our lives.

"You want some popcorn?" she asked suddenly.

"Sure." I pulled myself back to the present to answer. Thought I was probably doing as well as anybody else whose dad had just died.

But by the time she brought out the popcorn, my mind had already found a new thought. It was a possibility for the future for me to consider. It was new to me, and different. So different that I didn't dare mention it to anyone else. It ended with . . . *what if I'm not able to mother this baby?* It was too desperate a possibility. But I had wanted books only about the baby growing. About what was happening inside my body. Not about how to take care of a newborn. Much less about when he or she was no longer a baby. Even Mrs. Horn was having a hard time and she was dean of a college. Good grief! How would I cope with somebody who shoved over tables because he missed having a father?

I didn't even want to look at the new thought that had come, so I pushed it aside quickly and thought instead of how it was to live with Uncle Mac and Lacey. Took a look at the long spring months stretching ahead. I'd make myself be a mother. I could control my own life. A person can force herself if necessary.

I found out different. My safety valves were hidden. I suddenly started dreaming of Nicholas Canton and the smell of his skin and the sound of his breathing when he had kissed me. And because a person's safety valves are sometimes stronger than willpower, I couldn't shake him from my mind at night when it was dark and my defenses were down. Maybe it was because a second desperate thought had wedged its way through a crack in the door of my mind. Maybe there'd never be anybody else for me my whole life through. Maybe he was it.

29

WHO KNEW THAT MY ROOMMATE WOULDN'T WANT to wait until July sixteenth. Along about mid-April I began to have light contractions. My beach ball of a stomach hardened like a huge rock. False labor, my doctor called it. Not serious. Then, in early May, came cool weather again and harder contractions. "To bed with you!" That's what the doctor said.

"Blackberry winter," Aunt Lacey called our cold May days. *So, what do you call an out-of-season birth trying to happen?* I wondered. And why couldn't I bend the way I used to? And my fingers were swollen, not to mention my belly and feet.

One day while Mac and Lacey were at work and Cindy and Cliff at school, their mom came knocking at the patio door.

"Oh, hi," I said after I'd pulled the heavy drape to one

side a slit to see who'd be knocking at the back of the house on a Wednesday afternoon. "Come on in."

She was breathless and rosy-cheeked from her walk across the two back yards on this cool, late-spring day. She carried a makeshift tray, a box lid. "I came home for lunch and thought I'd share. Have you eaten lunch yet?"

"No. No, I haven't."

"Go, go, go! Get back in bed, I know you're supposed to be chained to your bed. Cindy told me. I just made some vichyssoise. . . ."

"Vichyssoise? I've never heard of that." It sounded foreign.

"It's just fancy for potato soup. It's usually served cold, but I warmed ours for this chilly weather. I hope you like it."

I did like it. It was hot and seasoned and smooth. Even though I wasn't actually sick, it felt good to be pampered.

"Potatoes always taste good to me," she said after we'd finished. "They sort of satisfy a basic hunger. You know?"

Mrs. Horn was about Aunt Lacey's age, I was guessing. Late thirties or early forties. She acted young. The way she clasped her hands around her knees and hugged them. The way she dressed, wearing knee socks like she was one of the coeds at the college. And her smile was young, too. Quick and young for a person who'd faced some of the things she'd been up against.

"I'll bet it gets lonely in bed all day, huh?"

"Yes, it does. Aunt Lacey checked out books for me

from the library, but you can only read just so long before you go cross-eyed."

She nodded. "I know. I know."

Then we sat in silence. I wanted her to stay. It was so good for another person to be in the house. "What made you think about coming with soup?" I asked her.

"Oh . . . it was almost lunchtime and I was getting hungry . . ."

"It was so good," I said. I wanted to ask her questions about how she got to be dean of women in a college. Well, to be truthful . . . also questions about the prisoner-of-war camp. Maybe she learned how to make potato soup while she was there. I thought I'd ask, "Where'd you learn to make it? The potato soup?" That was safe. If she wanted to talk about it, she would; if not, no.

"Oh, I learned how to make potato soup a long time ago . . ."

That wasn't quite enough for me. Oh, well . . . here was the plunge. I was taking it. "When you were in the Philippines?"

She looked up, startled.

"Cindy told me a little about that." I didn't want to get Cindy in hot water.

"Yes. As a matter of fact that *was* when. A shipload of potatoes came to the island and we were given those for our food supply, while they lasted."

Then she opened up. Told me everything. She told me

what it was like to live in a mud-floored shelter. To wear the same clothes every day. When she got to the part about birthing a set of twins in that forsaken spot, she said it had been easier than she'd thought it would be. "Raymond was there to help. And though he'd been injured, he could still help. Any help was better than none, you know."

"I'm sorry he didn't live," I said. "That must have been awful."

"It was. Oh, we were prepared to face hard times. Even before we were captured. I had signed up to be part of the medical staff, to support our country by taking care of its soldiers on foreign soil. Then I met Raymond. He stood for everything good and right that I also believed in. We felt we were on a mission together. Even after we were captured we felt that way."

She sat silent a long time before she went on. I studied her streaked blond hair. The smattering of freckles on her face she tried to hide with powder. She didn't notice me watching her, though. She was back on that island. "I haven't talked about this in quite a while. I began digging his grave back in a thicket before he died because I knew it would take me days. And nursing two babies made me weak."

I tried to picture it, the day he died. First feeding the babies so they wouldn't cry. Then, small as she was, dragging his body to the hole she'd dug.

"I had to take his clothes," she added, "for cloths to

wipe with. We had no diapers, so the babies wore only tops I fashioned."

She'd left that island after peace was declared. Left with two babies and nothing else she could carry in her hands. What she learned, I guessed, she'd carried inside.

"When the war was over we came back to the States, but I no longer wanted to be a nurse. My parents helped me as I went back to the university, and here we are."

I smiled at her. "Didn't you ever want to marry again?" I asked. Here was a question near to my heart.

She shook her head. "No. Didn't feel the need to search for anyone else."

After she left, taking her box lid with the two empty bowls in it, I lay in bed and thought about Mrs. Horn's story. I began to believe courage needn't be big, after all. Sometimes courage could be as small a thing as sticking a pin in the shell of a raw egg and naming it "supper."

30

WHEN I WOKE AND LOOKED AT THE LUMINOUS numbers on the face of my clock, it read 5:30. Awful early of a July morning for me to be this wide awake. I turned over in the bed and pulled a pillow over my head so when Mac got up about 5:45 I wouldn't wake back—whoa! What was that? The cramp of all cramps in my back? I groaned into it until it let up.

I knew exactly what it was. Unlike the light contractions I'd been battling, this one meant business.

I swung my legs over the side of the bed and sat up. Totally awake now. No chance to snooze. It was sort of scary the way that contraction had taken hold of my body. If you have a foot cramp, you stand up and it eases off. Not this feeling. It was in a different league.

I waited, sitting there on the edge of the bed, and then

it came again after a bit. I looked at the clock. It said 5:38. Eight minutes since the first one.

When Mac came down to the kitchen at 5:45, I went on up to have a cup of coffee with him. Didn't have to tell him either. I'd no more than sat at the bar when a third wave hit and I hung on tight to the edge of the bar until it passed.

"O-o-o-oh, buddy!" he said from across the kitchen, frozen with the full coffee scoop halfway to the coffee maker. "I'd better be waking Lacey."

"How often are the contractions coming?" she whispered through a smile from ear to ear, her pink rubber curlers poking every which way in her hair. "Are we having this baby this morning?"

"Eight minutes," I told her. "And maybe."

But the contractions stayed eight minutes apart all morning long. Lying down, standing, walking. Eight minutes. Mac called every half hour from the newspaper office and Lacey stayed right near the phone to tell him, "Status quo."

I got so hungry I ate a bowl of Cheerios. Then the contractions cut to five minutes and got harder and Lacey called the doctor.

"Let's go," she said, putting the phone back in its place, and she whisked through the house gathering, dropping, closing. We threw on our clothes, and she hauled my suitcase from under my bed, where it had lain, packed for weeks.

At the hospital, the nurse told Lacey she'd take me on back to the labor room and, while she was telling her, another contraction seized me right there in the front hall, and I hung on to a gurney that was sitting over to one side.

"Come on back this way, hon," the nurse told me when it was done. "We'll get you to undress and we'll prep you and call the doctor and—good grief! You're not having another one, are you?"

I nodded because there was no voice in me with this swift and powerful surge.

She did let me get through it and then we tore down the hall to the labor room, with me waddling as fast as I could. "She's less than a minute apart!" she called to a plump nurse who was getting a bed ready. "Call the doctor!"

Maybe there were only two nurses. Seemed like eight or ten. They whirled around me. I may have been scared but I wasn't lonely. Didn't have time to be. And those contractions lifted me from the labor bed so only my head and my heels were on a solid surface.

"Welcome . . . Welcome." It was the first nurse. "See if you can shift over to this gurney. Help us out here, hon."

I did my best and hadn't put all my weight down good before they were rolling me down the hall and through the doors of the delivery room.

Bursting through those doors. Leaving an old way of living behind. Launching from this planet called Earth into a whole different solar system.

It was cold. Outside it was summer. I could see the sky through the windows that surrounded this circular room. Windows even in the ceiling. But in here it was cold.

Two nurses were helping me onto the delivery table but it wasn't as hard as a regular table. It was sort of soft and comfortable when I wasn't in a contraction. And someone laid a warmed white blanket over me.

A nurse with a mask suddenly appeared at my head. To my right.

"On the next contraction," she said, and her words sifted through her gauze mask, "we're going to give you a little relief with this rubber mask I'll be putting over your face. Just breathe deep with it, honey."

"Here comes one," I said and she clamped the mask to my face. I couldn't breathe and I struggled against it. Then I had to breathe and, mixed in with the rubber smell, there was another smell, and I slept with that one.

I woke when she removed the mask and we waited. Dr. Nokes came in. Mask. Gloves. Green surgical gown. Another contraction.

"Welcome." I struggled out of my brief nap. "What're you going to name this baby?" he asked.

"Adam." My mouth was so dry I could hardly form the word.

"And if it's a girl?" He pushed down on my abdomen.

"Don't know."

The contraction came again, and I pulled for the mask because the pain was so engulfing. As I sank with the gas

I was reminded of the tide. Of the ocean rolling. Of the tremendous power of the sea. And of contractions seizing a baby and thrusting it into the world.

I rose again to this windowed room just long enough to feel a splash of warm liquid hit my legs and I saw Dr. Nokes motion with his hand and the rubber mask came to my face for good and I left.

"Mrs. O'Neal. Mrs. O'Neal. Wake up now. Can you hear me?"

I was in a hallway. It was a woman's voice. Where was she?

"Do you want to see your baby, Mrs. O'Neal?"

Who is she talking to? Mrs. O'Neal? Where did she come up with that name? Is my mother here? Standing where I can't see her?

"Here's your baby."

I looked to my left. And as I focused, something blue came near. It was a blanket. And now there was a face. Eyes closed. Just small horizontal lines actually. Pink face. Wrinkled as leaf lettuce but almost scalded looking, it was so rosy. Dark, short hair.

Suddenly it moved. Stretched back and grimaced its face. Opened its mouth and said its first word. "Laa-aa-aa-aa." Not *la* as in do-re-me-fa-so-*la*. But *laa* as the first part of *lamb*.

"It's a little boy," the nurse whispered.

The hand I reached out to touch with had a needle in

it, and the nurse told me to use my other hand. "You're receiving blood in that arm," she said.

"Blood?"

"Yes, hon. You hemorrhaged. We like to lost you. He's a pretty big 'un for somebody as small as you. Seven pounds, eight ounces. Twenty-one inches long, too."

Lost me? Wouldn't *that* have been something. To be bringing in new life and somehow get lost in the struggle.

I reached the other hand and touched my son's face. And when I did, he turned his head quick to my touch and tried to nurse it.

"Not yet, young man," the nurse told him. "I'll take you to your mama in a little while. Let her rest now. What're you going to name him?" she asked me before she left and at that moment he was no longer an "it" but became a person.

"Adam," I told her. "Adam for a friend. Walter for my daddy. Adam Walter."

Aunt Lacey had been the first to come. Right after he'd been born and I was back in my room. Then Mac and the Horns. Even Cliff. By nightfall everybody I knew in Virginia had already come and discussed if he had my nose, feet, hair, hands, toes. Mama and Evelyn Sue called to say they were coming tomorrow.

Me? I was trying to see if there was any of Randy in this baby. That was when everybody had left and I had the baby with me. They'd only seen him through the nursery

183

window. I could look up close. Feel his doe-smooth skin. Watch him look at my face and know I was just a blur yet.

"Adam," I whispered, "I'm your mother." Nothing like trying the name on for size.

After they took him to the nursery, way into the night, I lay in my semiprivate room and listened to the sounds of my own happiness beating with my heart, just down the hall from where my son slept, his small heart beating out the beginnings of its long rhythms of life on Earth.

"Could you turn out your light?" Mrs. Decker, the woman in the other bed, asked sometime after midnight.

"Sure," I said as I pulled the string. Then, lying in the dark, I floated along, planning my life. Trying to figure if I could do what I needed to do and be the mother Adam needed.

31

NURSING A BABY CAN BE HARD. NOT IMPOSSIBLE, BUT hard. The pediatrician and Adam decided he wasn't getting enough from me, so we started supplementing with several bottles of formula a day two days after we got home from the hospital. Then what milk I had dried up and we went totally to formula. It irked me because there was one more expense for Lacey and Mac. I'd thought I could at least take care of that myself.

He slept three hours at the most, then screamed at the top of his lungs for more formula. Babies don't always smell good, aren't always quiet, are heavier in your arms than you'd think. And they're in your arms an awful lot of the time. And you love holding this new baby. But not for hours.

Mama and Evelyn Sue came and stayed until after we got home from the hospital. Two days later, the day they left, Mama slipped me a fifty-dollar bill. "Just a little something now and I'll send more later," she whispered. "Welcome, you know you could come back to Lily if you wanted to?" She looked at me with her pinpoint eyes, making sure I knew she meant it.

"Could I, Mama? I mean really, could I? Would Adam ever be accepted in Lily? What would we tell people? Would it be fair to him?"

We sat in silent knowledge of truth as opposed to wishes.

"No, I'd better look for a part-time job here," I told her.

"Now don't you go to work too soon," she hastened to say, tucking the fifty into my slacks pocket.

"I won't," I promised. And we dropped the subject.

I showed Evelyn Sue how to pin on cloth diapers. "See, here . . . you fold it this way. All the while, though, you've got to be thinking, since it's a boy, the thickness has to be in front."

She watched me sponge bathe him and oil him up good, then powder his bottom and diaper him. And so did Adam, watch me. He didn't protest his bath. Just watched as I went through it all. Only afterwards he began to fuss, and I showed Evelyn Sue how to hold the bottle tall so he didn't get air.

"Burp him after every ounce," I told her, and then I lay down on the bed to watch her. Losing all that blood had made me weak. Felt like somebody had taken an axe to between my shoulder blades.

"You're lucky, Welcome," Evelyn Sue said when she

put Adam to her shoulder to burp him. Not like Hattie Mercer had shown me but I let her go on with it. Was too tired to explain the better-under-the-arms way to her.

"Why so? Why am I lucky?"

"Some people don't ever get the chance to have their own baby. Always just borrowing somebody else's. You know?"

I didn't answer. I didn't feel lucky. I just felt worn slam out. Night feedings. Weak from the loss of blood. Washing diapers. Hanging them out.

"Take Aunt Lacey," Evelyn Sue continued. Adam burped and she went back to feeding him his bottle. "She's never known about this."

"I know," I said and closed my eyes and thought about what I needed to do for Adam and for me. "I know."

We had Q-Tips and cotton balls, baby powder and baby oil. Diapers. Undershirts. Everything a person would need for a baby. What was missing was too huge to name. At first.

32

EVERY DAY ADAM CAME A LITTLE CLOSER TO BEING A person to me. He watched me with his round, dark eyes. He was a watchful baby. Not a fusser except when he was hungry. A watcher.

The Horns came daily. With food. With gifts. It was almost like they adopted us. Cindy held Adam the entire time she was there. Wouldn't let Cliff hold him. "Women know about these things," she told him. Cliff looked relieved. Probably didn't want to hold him. I could see by the look on Cindy's face she was falling in love with Adam. Wanted him for her own. And I understood the feeling. I loved him, too. But she wouldn't have doted on him so if she'd had all the upkeep that goes along with having a baby. She'd have been too tired to work up enough energy to dote.

Hattie Mercer came when Adam was two and a half

weeks old. All the way from Raleigh, North Carolina. I'd written to her when I was in the hospital. She had a cousin in Norfolk she spent the night with and they drove out on Friday afternoon and stayed for supper.

I let Hattie be the first to read to him out of the nursery rhyme book she'd sent him.

"'Baa, baa black sheep, have you any wool . . . ?'"

Her voice floated up to me as I made formula in the kitchen. Boiled the water. Boiled the bottles with their narrow necks and the nipples. Inside the sterilizer. Mixed the formula and poured it through a funnel, had boiled the formula water, too. And the funnel. Poured the formula into each bottle. Six ounces now. He'd moved up from four ounces a feeding to six now and burped only once halfway through the bottle. Things changed almost daily.

Adam and I went for a stroll every day just after breakfast, when it wasn't so hot yet. And I could feel myself slowly getting stronger because of those walks. And due to the iron pills Lacey bought for me to take to build back my blood.

Still in all, I rested when Adam did for the most part. I was going to need my strength as he grew. I was going to need my strength for being a mother.

Evelyn Sue sent letters of encouragement and Mama kept up her Saturday calls, catching me up on Lily.

Even when I rested, I pondered about my life, now that Adam was born. I didn't want to spend it skating to cars with trays of food. I wanted to do more than that for the rest of my life. But if I stayed here with Lacey and Mac, I'd have to go to work soon. I just couldn't freeload much longer.

I could have gone crazy trying to decide what to do. I finally told myself I'd know exactly what to do when it came time. The day would arrive and I'd just know. I hoped that was the truth.

Part of me heard a voice saying I was sixteen and didn't want sterilizing bottles, boiling water, making formula, washing diapers. But then, does anybody really want that? I was being honest with myself here when I admitted that. But there was a lot about Adam I needed, that held me. Maybe he was the first person in the world who ever needed *me*. But the question, the *real* question was, could I give him enough of what *he* needed? It came up at supper one night.

I passed Lacey a bowl of lima beans and that long stream of pent-up thoughts began to unwind right out of me. "I think I'd better begin looking for a part-time job," I blurted after I'd laid out a few of my worries.

Lacey's eyes locked with mine over the steaming vegetables.

"I know," I continued, "it'll be hard, but maybe I can work when you're home to baby-sit Adam."

She said nothing. Just took the bowl, helped herself, and passed it on to Mac, who was uncharacteristically silent. I heard Adam whimper in his sleep as he lay in his playpen in the living room.

"That way I could help with the finances."

Lacey forked a small group of beans but didn't make it to her mouth with them. She looked first at Mac, then at me. "I try not to interfere, to step in before I'm asked. But look, Welcome, try this scenario on for size. You are walking home from the doctor's office and you pass a house that's on fire. You can see the smoke, the flames. What do you do? Grab the garden hose and try to put out the fire? No, you call the fire department and alert the people in the house if possible, and the neighbors."

Uncle Mac grunted at her to stop and she did. We just ate in silence while I played around with her story inside my head.

Finally I asked, "What's the fire?"

"Life," she popped back. "School clothes, money for Boy Scouts and camping gear, enough to live on without worrying about where next week's groceries will come from, money to pay a doctor, college . . ."

I thought that through. "And a part-time job is the garden hose?"

She nodded.

Uncle Mac asked for the butter. I passed it. Almost. The dish was greasy and it slipped. Fell hard on the table and split right in two. Right in front of him. I saw four pieces, though, through the tears that sprang so suddenly they took me by surprise.

"I'm so sorry," I whispered. Had been proud I hadn't broken a dish all that time I'd been living with them. Until tonight.

"Don't you worry about that, Welcome," Uncle Mac tried to reassure me. "It's only a butter dish."

But it was much more than a butter dish. It was Aunt Lacey's fire I was seeing. And I knew for a fact a garden hose wasn't going to be enough.

Aunt Lacey patted my hand and looked so concerned, I had to say it wasn't only the dish, though I was sorry for breaking it.

"What can I do?" I asked, meaning about the fire, about life.

She knew exactly what I meant. "Go back to school; don't work yet. Go."

It was short. She wasn't wordy. Just four words really, but I heard them all night in my sleep. *Go back to school.* She did add one more thought: "There are seasons of life for things, events. You're in spring trying to stretch to summer, Welcome. It's too soon."

I slept that night ever aware of this decision facing me. An edge I had to negotiate soon one way or the other. Ever aware of how much I loved this small boy breathing evenly in his crib not five feet from my bed.

It was bath time two days later, before his late-night bottle. I was talking along to him, saying nursery rhymes as Hattie had told me to do, and Lacey was watching. Waiting with a towel to bundle him in. I noticed what were narrow chores for me were wide joys for Lacey. Maybe what was missing was the readiness. I hadn't lived long enough to miss this yet, while she'd been ready for a baby for so long it was a deep drink after years of being thirsty.

What had I done? Bringing a new life into mine, only to find I didn't run deep enough yet. Loving a person and taking responsibility for him are two separate acts. The first I owned in spades. The latter was beyond me.

I trickled water from my fingers over his tummy and smiled at his round eyes as he felt the warm water. Suddenly, no warning at all, he cracked a toothless grin. Really wide. And cooed a first small sound. Lacey laughed out loud. Not me. I stepped back from it. Lacey didn't even notice, because I held it all inside me and she was so full of Adam and his connecting.

But for me, that was when. If I stayed one more day, I'd be sunk and hooked in love with Adam, grinning his first grin up into my face. If I were to receive another smile he let loose, I might not be able to go.

"I think I need to go back to Lily," I told Lacey, casual like, while I slipped Adam into his nightgown. "Would Adam be all right with you?" I looked up quick. "I mean, would you be all right with him here?" I laughed. Laughed! I couldn't believe that fell out of my mouth . . . the laugh. It was the mistake I'd made in asking if Adam would be all right and, then in trying to correct it, and to keep from crying, the wrong emotion flew up.

Lacey placed her hand on his tummy to hold him steady on my bed when I laid him back down. To keep him from rolling right off onto the floor and from jerking with that fear of falling babies suddenly have. "We could make it work, Welcome," she said. "It'll be all right." I knew at that moment she'd understood the laugh. Lacey knew. She knew I didn't think this was funny.

I stood, looking down at Adam. I didn't want to leave him. I didn't think I could stay with him.

"Who would I be to him? To Adam? If I leave."

She put her free arm around my shoulders and squeezed. "Whatever you decide. We'll go along with your choice. You could be his mother still, or his 'aunt,' or just his friend. But remember, if you choose to be his mother, the repercussions of his not having a father may haunt you. And him. Just be aware of that. It's your choice to make, Welcome."

"I'll have to think about it," I told her, but I didn't pull away from her arm. It felt so good to know I was understood.

"When would you go?" Lacey asked.

"Tomorrow," I shot back without hesitation. That much I was sure of. The sooner the better. No more smiles.

"How long would you stay?"

"I don't know." And I really didn't. Could be for a year and a half. Could be forever.

She nodded. "I'll be able to stay home with him until we find someone to come part-time when I'm at school. It'll be all right."

She kept saying those two words. *All right.* Nothing is ever *all right.* Not all of it, right. Just some of it. I hoped enough of it.

So, as soon as the house was quiet, I wrote a letter to Adam. Told him how I'd been counting on all that I'd teach him, come the right time. Like how to brush his teeth in little round circles, not up and down. And roller-skate, how to balance. I'd even thought ahead to his first day of school and how I'd put him on the bus that squealed to a halt out in front of the house every school day morning.

Then I fed him a bottle and I rubbed the top of his head and looked into his eyes that he turned up to watch me.

"Things I counted on teaching you, baby . . . it's not going to happen."

A sadness deep as forever came upon me and I caught myself to keep back a sob that had wrenched itself loose.

I didn't tell him any more. Just watched him as he finished up and, after I burped him, I laid him back down. And waited for sleep to come to me. Not deep, though, because I was awake to hear Mac's alarm clock go off and his heavy feet hit the floor overhead. I got up, too. Dressed. Packed. Kept as quiet as night. Went up to the kitchen to have a cup of coffee with Mac.

He smiled and hugged me up. When I pulled out of his hug, he lifted my chin and said, "It's all gonna work out, Welcome."

If one more person told me it would work out, would be all right, I thought I'd scream. Nobody knows if it will. That's the chance you take. I was taking. I nodded at Mac though, like I believed it.

"There's a bus at seven-forty-five and one at ten and . . ."

"Seven-forty-five," I said.

"We'll need to get on the road then. I'll get Lacey."

I swallowed the rest of the hot, sweet coffee, then tip-toed down the stairs. Didn't want to wake Adam. I tucked my letter to him in his sock and undershirt drawer. Some-day he'd be old enough to read it. Someday maybe I'd be back in his life able to do more.

I grabbed my suitcase and purse. Then I went back for one last look. Adam was lying asleep on his back, his hands to either side of his head, open but curled. Now and again his mouth nursed air and then he slept quiet.

"Adam," I said good and low so he'd not waken now. I couldn't have stood that. "I can't do for you what you need."

His even breathing kept right on, bridging this change he would never remember and I would never forget.

"Good-bye," I whispered. "Adam. Your Aunt Lacey and Uncle Mac will take better care of you than I can for now. This is not easy."

I turned to go upstairs. "I love you, Adam O'Neal," I said out loud, my back to him. "I love you this much." His even breathing answered me back.

Then I left.

What I carried with me that lasted was a small black-and-white photograph with Lacey holding him. That and his first smile.

It was a day and a half before the scent of baby powder left my skin.

Part Three

O'Neal
421 W. Main St.
Lily, N.C. 27889

Mr. & Mrs. Mac Hall
Master Adam O'Neal Hall
435 Gotham Road
Virginia Beach, VA 23455

The Faculty and Graduating Class
of
The University of North Carolina
School of Medicine
request the honor of your presence
at the Commencement Exercises
on Friday evening, May Twenty-fourth
One Thousand Nine Hundred Sixty-eight
at seven o'clock
Kenan Stadium,
Chapel Hill, North Carolina

WELCOME MARIE O'NEAL, M.D.

Adam, Hope you can come.
Your best buddy, Welcome